A
CLUTCH
OF
FABLES

BOOKS BY TEO SAVORY

NOVELS

Landscape of Dreams, *New York*, 1960
The Single Secret, *New York*, 1961; *London*, 1962
A Penny for the Guy, *London*, 1963; *New York*, 1964
To A High Place, *Santa Barbara*, 1972
Stonecrop: The Country I Remember, *Greensboro*, 1977

SHORT FICTION

A Clutch of Fables, *Greensboro*, 1977

POEMS

Traveler's Palm, 1967
Snow Vole, 1968
Transitions, 1973
Dragons of Mist and Torrent, 1974

TRANSLATIONS

ELEVEN VISITATIONS, katrina von hutten, *Munich*, 1971
(with Ursula Mahlendorf) THE CELL, Horst Bienek, *Santa Barbara*
and *Toronto*, 1972; *London*, 1974
SELECTED POEMS, Guillevic, *London* and *Baltimore*, 1973
EUCLIDIANS, Guillevic, *Greensboro*, 1975
(with Vo-Dinh) ZEN POEMS, Nhat Hanh, *Greensboro*, 1976

FOR THE UNICORN FRENCH SERIES

Supervielle, 1967
Corbière, 1967
Michaux, 1967
Queneau, 1971

Prévert I, 1967
Jammes, 1967
Prévert II, 1967
Guillevic, 1968

FOR THE UNICORN GERMAN SERIES

Günter Eich, 1971

TEO   SAVORY

A
CLUTCH
OF
FABLES

Nine Drawings by Emil Antonucci

Greensboro: Unicorn Press

LCC 73-76686
ISBN 0-87775-043-2, cloth
ISBN 0-87775-104-8, paper

Several fables were previously published, in *Prairie Schooner,*
Approach, Unicorn Journal and *Webster Review.* "The Monk's
Chimera" was included in the Avon anthology, *Imperial Messages:
100 Modern Parables* (1976), edited by Howard Schwartz, and in
the Pushcart Prize anthology, *Best of the Small Presses, Vol. 2,* (Push-
cart/Avon, 1977), edited by Bill Henderson; "The Silver Swan" will
be included in the second volume of *Imperial Messages* (Avon,
1978). All are reprinted with the kind permissions of the editors.

The fables were written between the years 1960 and 1974, in
New York, Mexico, California and Massachusetts; the earliest three,
"The Shaggies," "The Ants and the Grasshopper" and "Little Brown
Burros," in 1960; the most recent, "The Concept of the Cage" and
"Friends of the Song Sparrows," in 1973 and 1974.

Table of Contents

FOREWORD

Although there has been a revival of interest in short allegorical forms such as the parable, the fable, and the prose poem in recent years, there are still very few authors who have produced book-length collections of these works. Perhaps the least attempted of these forms is the fable, which is a short, allegorical story in which the central figures are animals. Of course, everyone is familiar with Aesop's fables, still the classics of the genre, which have served as models for every writer attempting to write a fable ever since. Some classic collections of fables derived from Aesop's model are those of LaFontaine, those of the medieval Jewish writer Berechiah ha-Nakdan (whose fables have been translated into English by Moses Hadas under the title of FABLES OF A JEWISH AESOP), and those of Hans Christian Andersen. In this century the masters of the art have been the Russian author Krilov and James Thurber, whose two collections revived the fable as a viable form in this country.

It was with considerable interest, then, that I approached this book-length collection of fables by Teo Savory. Ms. Savory has already established herself as an accomplished writer of novels and poetry, and is an excellent and prolific translator from the French, German, and Vietnamese. Nothing in this background, however, suggests a proficiency at fables, and so it is a pleasure to find that A CLUTCH OF FABLES is a supremely accomplished collection, of remarkable range, in which echoes can be heard of all the prior masters of the fable, presented in the distinct speaking-voice of a teller of tales.

Unlike her predecessors, Ms. Savory does not settle for a single point of view, such as the all-knowing, down to earth tone of Aesop, or the sly, ironic, and often cynical voice of Thurber, but each of her fables manages to strike precisely the right balance of innocence and irony. In "The Monk's Chimera," for instance, the reader cannot but feel protective toward the poor monk who must explain to his Abbot how his conversation with a formerly stone griffin, who also happened to be "a godless monster," has caused it to take wing. Then there are fables such as "The Silver Swan," who "sings a song of unearthly beauty, but only once in her life, at the time of her death." Against all the odds this fable manages to be moving without any intrusion of the irony that a lesser author could not have kept out; it is a short masterpiece worthy of Hans Christian Andersen at his best. And at the other end of the spectrum there are fables such as "The Alley Cat and the Laws of Status" that burn with honest indignation, with a biting quality that even surpasses Thurber.

The twenty fables in this book were written over a fourteen year period, in various places, and this fact partly explains their diversity and also suggests how rare is the inspiration required to successfully write a new fable. The nine illustrations by Emil Antonucci, like the fables they illustrate, are appropriate and original without being in the least imitative of Thurber's or anyone else's. For all of these reasons A CLUTCH OF FABLES is a very unusual book that deserves the attention of those interested in how the fable, a two thousand year old literary form, has not only managed to survive, but also, on occasion, to thrive.

Howard Schwartz

A
CLUTCH
OF
FABLES

The Monk's Chimera

When the abbey was built, an old griffin came to perch on one of the flying buttresses. For centuries he sat there, watching the monks from his lidless eyes. After observing them for several generations, he realized that they never did anything different: prayers and penance, penance and prayers, the livelong day and half the night. True, there was some rather fine Gregorian chant coming out of the chapel, but after a few decades practice made it too perfect to be of interest. There was, of course, the activity in the distillery, after the lay brothers had gathered herbs in the meadows, when the monks made their profitable liqueur. But even that became, over the years, monotonously ambrosial. The griffin grew so bored he almost turned to stone.

He was thinking of flying back to Assyria when the mountebank, ragged and weary, arrived at the gates, breaking the even tenor of *ennui*.

The world of the open road and village square at carnival had not treated this poor fellow well. After finding haven with the monks, he stayed on, the humblest of the humble lay brothers. Then there was nothing of further interest until, one day, the griffin witnessed the miracle which occurred when the mountebank performed his juggling act for Our Lady. As we all know, the monks, educated persons of distinguished lineage, were able to offer up to her the fruits of their erudition, skill and industry, whereas this beggarly strolling player had nothing but an orange to balance on his nose while tossing two other oranges in the air —an indifferent act at best which this poor fellow, so the griffin thought, but indifferently performed. However, his lowly offering had evidently pleased Our Lady and she had smiled upon the mountebank.

5

The monks, when the miracle was discovered, were astounded. It was plain to the griffin that their noses, though unencumbered by oranges, were out of joint. The abbot was wise enough to make the best of it; the mountbank was soon made a monk, and later, when the abbey fell upon hard times, its liquour having lost favor to that of a rival order, the new monk's accomplishment was put to good use. Previously the abbot had kept the mountebank's good tidings within the four walls of the cloisters. Now he let a few rumors seep out. On the following Sunday there was a small crowd from the nearby town, come to gape at the mountebank as he juggled for Our Lady. And soon there were large crowds, from town and city, weekdays as well as Sundays. Their offerings replenished the abbey's coffers, and the mountebank grew very tired. He searched for a solitary resting place, as far from the other monks, and from the scene of his labors, as could be found; by chance, the buttress he chose to lean upon was the one which the griffin occupied. One day the mountebank raised his eyes from the ground and, looking heavenward, cried out, "How long, O Lord?" But what he saw up there was not the Lord's benign countenance, or even the peaceful sky, but the griffin's stony gaze. "Who are you?" the mountebank asked in astonishment.

"*I* might better ask that question," replied the griffin "as I have lived here much longer than you have." He looked down his nose in a very superior way; still, he did not seem unfriendly and so the monk replied, "If you have lived here so long, perhaps you have seen my miracle?"

"Indeed, yes," the griffin answered. "You must be honored and happy."

"Honored, but not happy."

"Not happy?"

"No, worn out. It was bad enough having to do my act once a day, but now the crowds are so great I have to do it once an hour. Why, it's worse than working the Fairs. I'm worn out, I tell you." A bell rang. "Compline. If it's not one thing, it's another."

"Poor fellow." The griffin did not sound too sympathetic—certainly he did not look it, with that stony face of his. Still, he was more understanding than the monks. The mountebank fell into the habit of spending a few minutes each day in converse with the griffin. The griffin told him about his native perch, on a *ziggurat* beside the Tigris, while the mountebank recounted the adventures which befall a strolling player. Always these pleasant interludes were cut short by a bell, summoning the mountebank to prayers or to his labor of entertaining the public.

One day he said to the griffin, "Do you think it is quite right to make the Smile of Our Lady into a sideshow?"

"Right, wrong—it seems to be the way of your world," the griffin replied.

"But do you not feel that Brother Abbot is, well, exploiting the goodness of Our Lady a trifle?"

"It would not be the first time," the griffin said, suppressing a yawn.

The mountebank's voice dropped to a whisper. "Do you think God approves?" he asked.

"How should a *Griffin* know anything of God?" the griffin retorted in his superior way.

The mountebank's neck ached with craning upward, but he stood on tiptoe (though that did not bring him much nearer) and craned still more, staring at the griffin. "You sound like an unbeliever!" he whispered, frightened. He had never noticed before how monstrous the griffin looked. Who ever heard of a lion with *wings* . . .?

"The word can scarcely apply, for I am a Chimera," the griffin said.

"Is that a name for a heretic?" The mountebank shrank down in his sandals. "God will strike you dead!"

"As God did not make me," the griffin said, "he cannot unmake me."

The mountebank was terrified and began making signs of the

cross, wildly, into the air. "Begone, chimera!" he cried.

The griffin lashed his tail slightly. Boredom again, even from the mountebank! It was unbearable. Slowly he flapped his wings, grown heavy with so much perching, and right before the mountebank's astonished eyes, he flew away and disappeared over the edge of the horizon.

Brother Abbot had seen the mountebank in conversation with the griffin, and now not two days went by before its absence was noted. "What have you done with our griffin?" the abbot asked sharply.

The mountebank crossed himself. "He was a Godless monster," he whispered.

"Nonsense!" the abbot exclaimed. "He was part of our architecture."

When the papal legate came on a visit, Brother Abbot was severely reprimanded for losing a valued art-work. "You must ask Brother Mountebank about the disappearance," the abbot replied.

"Art-work?" the mountebank repeated in his uncultured way. "No, no. He was a chimera."

When the saintly head of the Order came to look into the matter, he accepted the mountebank's statement and soon it became known that what everyone thought they had seen had been but a chimera. Thus it came about that an ignorant mountebank gave a new meaning to a word, causing the griffin, from his more interesting perch in Paris, to break occasionally into sardonic laughter.

The Ants And The Grasshopper

Some ants in a long, winding line were returning to their home. A grasshopper sitting on a fallen leaf impeded their approach. When the leader stopped, all his followers stopped behind him. "Why are you sitting there like that?" the leader asked. "It's warm in the sun," the grasshopper answered. The sun burnished the bright green of his wings, dazzling the ant, whose black body looked, to the grasshopper, like a pair of winter-killed seeds. "Showing off," the ant said. "Vulgar fellow!"

The grasshopper whirred his wings but did not leave his comfortable leaf. "What have you got there?" he asked the leader-ant. "Why are you toiling through this hot summer afternoon?"

"Fool! We're building our shelter." The grasshopper noticed then that each ant was carrying a portion of a twig. "Why shelter in the summer?" he asked with a yawn.

The ant dropped his bit of twig in exasperation. "Where are your eyes?" he asked. "Don't you see that all the anthills on the other side of the swamp have been destroyed? Didn't you hear the crows' news at dawn?"

"I was asleep," the grasshopper answered. "What was the news?"

"Wild boars are invading!" the ant cried.

"Never heard of them."

"Fool! They're at war with the woodchucks, and they kill all in their way, scorching the earth as they go. They snap crickets and grasshoppers out of the air, and stamp out ants with their monstrous hoofs."

"I can fly above them," the grasshopper said, "if I have to." He looked at the long line of ants thoughtfully. "But what can *you* do?"

9

If the sun hadn't been so warm, he might have offered to carry one or two on his back.

"Build shelters, of course," the ant replied. He picked up his bit of twig and signaled to his followers. They began to plod around the grasshopper's leaf toward the shelter they were building.

As the leaf was sun-drenched throughout the day, the grasshopper remained on it, amusing himself by watching the labors of the ants. All day they toiled, leveling off their hill, tunneling out the ground, then covering the hole with twigs. And all day they were forced to make a detour around the grasshopper. They did this without grumbling, though at times their leader called out derisive comments, such as: "Fool! No thought for the morrow," or, "You'll regret your feckless ways tonight."

At sunset the crows flew overhead, cawing a warning on their way to the top of the mountain. The leaf grew chilly and the grasshopper began to wonder uneasily about the wild boars. What were they? What would they do? Perhaps it would be wise to fly into the adjacent lilac bush. But before he could do so, he heard a thunderous crashing and snorting at the far side of the swamp. The last of the long line of ants scuttled into the new, underground shelter, pulling the last bit of twig firmly over his head as he disappeared. The terrible sounds grew nearer and the earth shook under the stamping of hoofs. Tongues of fire lit up the swamp. Looking about him, considering the branches of the lilac bush, the grasshopper was distracted by the sight of frenzied activity in a neighboring ant colony. These ants, too, had been working all day, but they had been unable to finish their shelter: their hill was but half leveled, and their twigs were lying in confusion beside it. Now they were pouring out of their home and making tracks toward the nearby, completed shelter. They scrabbled frantically at the twigs there, but before their feeble legs could scrape an entrance, a twig was removed from below and the ants who had built the shelter began to bombard their neighbors with pellets of dirt, wood and gravel. However, the neighbor-ants were so determined to get into the shelter that, ignoring their wounded brothers and leaving their dead heaped on the ground, they forced their way though the small entrance, killing the guards as they did so. The grasshopper observed the battle of the ants from above. The roof of the shelter cracked and heaved, finally blowing into the air as though from a subterranean explosion, and the shelter, which the ants had toiled to build, became a mere hole in the ground, exposed to the sky and all creatures beneath it. The hole was filled with the dead and dying. At the same time, the wild boars were approaching. Their hoof-beats shook the earth to its core, their jaws crunched branch and animal alike, and the fire from their nostrils burned brighter than the noon sun.

The only ant now not dead of his wounds was the leader and he, of a certainty, would not last long. The grasshopper whirred his wings and rose in the air. The ant looked up at him. "Fool!" he cried feebly. As the fire from the wild boars' nostrils burned, in an instant, the lilac bush, and began to singe the grasshopper's wings, he flew as high off the earth as he could, and as he felt his wings begin to crumple he said, "It is better to die out in the air."

The Alley Cat
And The Laws Of Status

One night a house-cat named Hurkle was taken ill with an acute attack of appendicitis. "An emergency!" Dr. Fox exclaimed. "To the hospital with him at once!" And he telephoned for an ambulance.

The cat was lifted from the ambulance into a wheel chair. His pain was becoming steadily worse and he was now doubled up with it. From time to time a howl escaped his lips. His life-long fear of surgery forgotten, he longed only for the operating room and an anaesthetic. But before he could be taken upstairs he had to wait in an office, howling the while, until an owl with a long piece of paper came in and began to question him.

Hurkle was very poor indeed at answering; aside from his own name, he seemed to know very little about himself, and to questions such as Religion . . . Blue Cross . . . Social Security Number . . . mother's maiden name, and so on, he only replied, "My gut hurts."

The owl threw up his talons in despair. "Pull yourself together or you'll never get admitted," he said. "Now then. Nearest relative?"

But the truth was Hurkle had no relatives, never *had* had any, being, sad to say, a foundling who had lived out his kittenhood under some cars on East Eighteenth Street, until one day a dachshund had nosed him out, but in a friendly way, and Hurkle had followed him home. Then he had lived in the vestibule of the dachshund's brownstone until, at last, he had been grudgingly admitted and grudgingly allowed to remain. Now he was grown up, an ill-adjusted and insecure bachelor.

"Nearest relative?" the owl repeated.

"Well, uh, Max the dachshund," the cat replied.

"I can't put down a thing like that," the owl said angrily.

"I can't help being an orphan." Hurkle gave a loud howl.

"It would look like miscegenation," the owl said. "Oh, well, I'll put down your doctor's name. Though it's most irregular."

Hurkle only howled the more. "I'll be glad when this night's over," the owl said. "Now, what sort of accommodation do you want?"

Max the dachshund had spent years trying to teach this cat how to get along in the world. "You've got two strikes against you to start with," he'd said. "First, you're an orphan, and secondly your hair is so short. Nothing we can do about *that*. But always remember that what all dogs and cats are interested in above anything else is status." Oddly enough, the analogy Max had most often used during his instruction was that of a hospital. "Life is a hierarchy," he would say. "It's like a hospital." (Max had been sickly as a pup and had never quite forgotten it.) "Some quadrupeds are in private rooms because they're born to them—like that Angora next door. Others are in semi-private, where they are quite comfortable—or could be except that they are always trying to get into private. Then there's the wards. No one from private ever goes there, and semi-privates wouldn't be caught dead in them."

"Whereabouts are you?" the ingenuous cat had asked.

The dachshund rested his long nose on one gleaming black paw. It was plain to be seen where *he* had been born.

"I see," said the cat. He looked at himself in the mirror. There was nothing reflected there that he could preen himself about. Not only was his hair appallingly short and with very little sheen to it, he was not even tiger-striped but, instead, white with patchy and rather pointless black markings, somewhat like a Holstein cow.

"Pure ward," the cat murmured at his reflection.

"Not necessarily," the dachshund said. "And not with me here to instruct you. For someone with your background, the only way is to learn your rights and insist upon them." He got off his pillow and gave an elongated stretch. "Even insist on some that you *haven't* got," he said. "For instance, it is now one and one-half hours until dinner. But it's a wise policy, occasionally, to insist on having it early." The dachshund began to bark— not his deep, watch-dog bark, but a shrill yapping. "Come on, howl!" he said. But the cat merely stood there, looking at his teacher with his mouth agape.

"I despair sometimes," the dachshund murmured, going back to his cushion.

"What's wrong with *being* ward if you *are* ward?" the cat asked.

"Everything." The dachshund closed his eyes.

"But then you don't have to worry about how to keep on staying in private or struggle to get there from semi-private," the cat said. "You can relax and enjoy yourself."

"Doing what?" the dachshund asked sleepily.

"Getting extra milk?"

"Purely for those in private."

Hurkle thought of several things, but realized that all had to do with privilege. "Well then," he said at last, "just roam around and catch a few butterflies."

"You want to be a beatnik or something?" The dachshund gave a delicate snore. "You'll see," he'd said. Then he'd gone to sleep.

Now the cat, twisted up with his pain and confused by the owl's questions, tried to remember some of Max's precepts. And so when the owl asked what kind of accommodation he wanted, the cat pulled himself together and said firmly, "Semi-private." There, that was a splendid compromise, he thought, and Max would be proud of his pupil.

The next day the cat was in post-operative coma for several hours and when he came to he was sick all over his bed. There were three other fellows in the room with him, howling in disgust. "When you want to do that, you ring for a basin," an Angora said. "The nurse brings it," a Persian said. The Siamese did not deign to speak at all but, instead, rang his bell. When the nurse came, he said, "I have no idea why I am in here with these—these creatures. But I refuse to remain with this latest addition."

The nurse was a deliciously young white rabbit with her cap worn at a daring angle. "We'll have you up in private tomorrow night, sir," she said, twitching one shell-pink ear in a flirtatious way.

"Straighten my sheets," the Siamese said coldly.

Posher than posh! Hurkle thought, gazing in awe at the Siamese. To be short-haired, yet even more aristocratic than an

Angora or Persian . . . . He called feebly to the nurse, "May I have a clean gown, please?" But she was busy patting the Siamese's pillows.

"Tomorrow night," he was saying, "is twenty-four hours too long. Either that one goes, or I do."

"That goes for me, too," said the Angora.

"And me," said the Persian.

Hurkle just lay there. Two tears rolled from his eyes, his belly hurt, and he felt nauseated again.

The nurse popped thermometers into the mouths of the Persian and the Angora. "You're semi-privates," she said firmly, "and here you'll stay." She looked angrily at Hurkle. "That alley cat can go to the ward."

In no time he was wheeled out of there and down to a camp-bed, hastily put up for him at the far end of a ward. No one changed his gown and he had missed evening wash during the move. The ward was a very noisy place as all the cats were constantly howling to get out of it and go up to semi-private and the nurse, instead of being a pretty white rabbit, was a very old duck with splayfeet. When Hurkle asked for a sip of milk she answered disagreeably, saying, "We'll have none of your trouble-making down here! Imagine," she told the rest of the ward, "this one got himself into semi-private and upset the whole hospital."

Hurkle could not sleep all night and in the morning was running a high temperature. Soon he was delirious. He dreamed he was a paw-loose kitten chasing butterflies, and once he thought he saw Max's soft-tipped long nose above him. On the third day, still in his soiled gown, tossing in his soiled cot, the cat breathed his last.

"He never once complained," the duck told Max, pretending a tear or two. "Never asked to go back to semi-private. A rough diamond, perhaps, but one of nature's gentlecats. Never any trouble."

"Never any trouble, eh?" Max repeated, looking at the corpse in its shoddy pine coffin.

There may be a worse place than a ward, but you are only put into it once.

The Lion's Tail

A lion who had seen better days lived in an old farmhouse with his wife. Each morning he shut the door of his studio and worked till dusk on his avant garde composition, *Atonal Fugues for Larynxes,* while his wife fed the chickens, weeded the vegetables, prepared the house for the weekend influx of lodgers, and ironed the lion's shirts. Though their circumstances were so straitened that, except for an old hen on feast-days, they had become vegetarians, the lion nevertheless continued to dress for dinner, or at least to change into a white shirt, as his ancestors had been wont to do, in the Egyptian desert, from time immemorial. At the height of the paying-guest season, when the lioness looked particularly exhausted and swollen-hocked, the lion would sigh and say, "How have we come to this?"

The answer, if one understands lions, was simple enough. On a nearby mountain top stood the summer quarters of a famed symphony orchestra with which the lion, in his youth, had begun his career in the first violin section. It had been expected that the lion, a prodigy as a cub, would quickly become concert master and, in time, conductor. The lion and his wife, then a frisky young tawny-head, had fallen in love with the wild landscape and purchased the old farmhouse. But, being lions, with lions' proud bearing and natural aloofness, they knew nothing of cocktail parties, flattery for board members, or dinner parties for lynxes from the critical journals; the lioness did not even own a low-cut blouse. And so the young lion was passed over while other cats—striped or spotted—moved up to the concert master's desk. And when the old Russian tiger died—dramatically, right in the middle of a tail-beat—his place was filled by a French poodle. And as the others moved up, the lion, no longer young now, moved back, until he was at the very last desk of the section, not even visible from some parts of the auditorium. The lion had borne his ignominy patiently, aided in his stoicism by

17

the thought of his compositions. While he played, perhaps, his part of *L'Après-midi d'un faune,* for the hundredth time, he could be thinking about his *Fantasia for Bull Fiddlers.* When this was finished and the triennial competition for works by orchestral members came about, hopes were high at the farmhouse. But again the lion was passed over. He grew chapfallen, slunk about the edges of the green-room like some common coyote or other brass player, and his fiddling fell off. "You must resign and devote yourself to composing," the lioness had said, not adding that he must resign before he was fired. Thus it came about that the farmhouse was turned into a lodging-house and the lioness, spouse to a King of Beasts, into a drudge.

One balmy June evening the lion felt festive. Putting on his old regimental tie, he went to the cellar and broke out a bottle of his grandfather's port. When the sparse and tasteless meal was done, he said, "We have something to celebrate, my dear. Today I completed number ninety-nine. We're on the home stretch."

The lioness needed no further explanation. She had long known that the *Fugues for Larynxes* were to number one hundred. She had a secret tally on a post out in the laundry shed, where she spent so much of her time, on which she kept count of her husband's progress.

"Bravo!" she cried. After a suitable pause she added, "I too have some news." Her husband noticed then that her whiskers were shining and that she'd combed her mane. "Old Pussy-foot," she said, referring to the manager of the orchestra, "is retiring and an up-and-coming youngster from Tanbark Business School is replacing him."

"Indeed?" the lion replied dubiously. "I do not know what a Business School has to offer music . . ."

"He's a musician himself," the lioness said, "in an amateur way, and most charming."

"You appear to know a good deal about him."

"I do. For my real news is this: he is coming here to live!" Her tawny eyes sparkled as though she were young again. "It will be a steady income and I won't have to take so many transients."

"Money," the lion muttered. "Always money!" His forebears had never mentioned the word. He straightened his whiskers after a moment. "What's this youngster's background?"

"Well," she replied hesitantly, "he's a lynx from the Bronx."

"A *lynx!*" A shudder shook the lion's gaunt but noble frame. "In this house? Never!"

The lioness put a restraining paw on her husband's pastern. He saw that she'd given herself a manicure. "He's not in the least like other lynxes," she said. "No malicious little *critiques* for 'Anti Musica' or 'The Deciduous Review'. No consorting with his own sex. Indeed, he's even engaged to be married to a charming young goose from Graduate Quacking School."

"Graduate School!" What had that to do with music . . . ? But his wife knew more about these modern matters than he did. Besides, as he looked at her manicured paw, he realized that the decision had been made.

"A lynx," he repeated. He pushed away his glass of port. Then he gave a roar to show who was, after all, still master. The rafters shook gratifyingly and his wife looked terrified. "Mind the weak joists, dear," she said.

The lynx moved in and the house brightened up. There was meat every night, flowers on the table, and the lioness had a new mane-do. The weekends, with fewer lodgers, were more peaceful. The lynx was good company, with a fund of orchestra gossip, and kept the lion well supplied with Chateauneuf du Pape and Coronas. The lion had to admit that life was much pleasanter. "He's a jolly good fellow," he told the lioness, "all that you said of him and more." Indeed, there was none of that slinking about, that lynx-eyed malice—and the young goose was amiable, giving only a token slap when the lion tweaked her pretty tail-feathers.

But the lioness received this praise without enthusiasm. "We'll see," she said darkly.

"You're getting fickle as a fitch!" the lion exclaimed.

"No, I'm not," she answered. "But haven't you noticed what's going on next door?"

"I did notice the place had been let this summer."

"It certainly has. To that ocelot from New York. He's con-

ducted there and in Paris, and now that the old poodle is retiring . . ."

"Retiring?"

"Don't you keep up with anything? This ocelot is sniffing
around our orchestra, and his house is full of lynxes—every
major critic in the country, as well as all those horses from Boston."

The next evening at cocktail time the lion posted himself on
the wall which separated the two properties. His wife was right,
as so often. Thoroughbred board members from Boston were
driven up by their chauffeurs; after they'd left, the lynxes from
New York arrived in their foreign sports cars. There were also
many willowy cubs of all sorts but only one sex; even, the old
lion was grieved to see, one or two lisping lion cubs. The ocelot,
whose tail-hairs seemed to have been bleached, lay languidly in
a deck-chair, a satin dressing-gown draped carelessly about him,
and held court. At about seven o'clock the young manager, their
lodger, drove up in his Tierwagen, accompanied by the four
Siamese whom the lion had seen swaying about the village in
scarlet jackets and platinum neckbands; they called themselves
the Smoky Quartet and played chamber music at select parties
of a notorious sort.

The lion gave a lusty roar and rushed into the house, where
his wife was cooking dinner.

"It's an orgy over there. I wouldn't soil your ears describing it."

"You needn't," she said, "as I've got eyes."

"It's Roman," he roared, "and you know what happened to
that empire."

The lioness began serving up the stew. "It's what will happen
to us that I'd like to know."

"Stew?" the lion observed—he had become used to steak this
summer. "And only for two?"

"*He* won't come home. He hasn't been home for four days—
how unobservant can you *be*—and the goose is up in her room
crying her eyes out."

Several days went by in gloom and wineless meals for two.
The goose had packed up and gone back to Graduate School,
and the young lynx came home only to change his clothes.

The lioness shook out her mane and said, "Two can play at this game." The competition for orchestral members' compositions would be judged within the fortnight, and the poodle's retirement had been officially announced. The lioness dusted off her address book and, taking up her pen, wrote to all her old friends on Upper Fifth Avenue and on Rittenhouse Square.

Worn out from his pleasures, the young lynx came home early for a nap and the lioness waylaid him. "You've been so charming to us," she said, "that we wish to do some small thing in return. We have invited some of our friends out to meet you." And she mentioned the names of some very famous old lions indeed—bankers, owners of oil companies and collections of Old Masters, and the entire board of directors of the Philadelphia Symphony Orchestra. The young lynx's eyes bulged.

"Well, I'm honored," he said.

"Dinner for twenty on Saturday. Black tie," the lioness said.

Two hens from the village polished the silver and were taught the rudiments of serving. The lioness prepared her menu well in advance—jellied consommé, venison à l'orgueil lyonnais, and Veldt pudding. Everything was ready and the lynx appeared in conservative dinner jacket before the first guests drove up. "May I help with the cocktails?" he asked politely.

"Not cocktails," the lioness said, switching her velvet train. "Sherry."

"Of course. Stupid of me."

"My husband is taking care of the wines, but you could help him," she said, nodding the three ostrich feathers on the top of her head.

"Only too pleased."

"Not with the wine," she said, "so much as with his peace of mind."

"Anything," the young lynx said. A Daimler was softly pulling into the driveway. "An honor," he added.

"It's the competition," the lioness whispered hastily. "You know how unworldly my husband is. He has completed his *chef d'oeuvre,* his one hundred Atonal Fugues. But I fear he does not even know how to enter the competition . . ."

"For orchestral members?"

"He is, after all, an *ex*-member."

"A mere technicality," the young lynx said, observing a black Lincoln brougham turning into the drive. "Easily overcome."

Stately lions in regally old-fashioned tailcoats, their wives in velvet gowns and pearl chokers, began slowly entering the farmhouse, while their zebras parked the gleaming black cars behind the chicken-runs and repaired to the potting-shed where a keg of beer had been broached for them.

The dinner went smoothly and afterwards the host was asked to play one or two of the fugues from his great work. The young lynx was approved for his quiet courtesy and modest manner. After the last guest had departed, the lion went outside to smoke a cigar, leaving his wife and their lodger with the dishes. As he approached the dividing wall he saw that his neighbor, the ocelot, and some of his gilded cubs, were standing on the other side of it. Giggling and batting daintily at each other in a drunken way, they were passing remarks on the lion's guests and whistling for their friend the lynx, who presently ran out of the lioness' kitchen and up to the wall. The lion secreted himself in a thicket to eavesdrop.

"Wasn't it the *most!*" the lynx said, preening himself.

The ocelot laughed. "Well, it was the funniest. All those old dodoes."

"Dodoes! They're the Four Hundred," the lynx retorted.

"Four hundred what?" the ocelot answered scornfully. "Hasbeens? They went out of style with horses' hats."

"*They* won't get you anywhere," said one of the Siamese, flashing his platinum neckband in the moonlight.

"No influence," added a mutant mink.

A favored fox-cub giggled. "Look what he's got on!" He pointed at the lynx's dark dinner jacket.

"As square as his friends, the lions," the ocelot agreed languidly. "Oh well, this will make a good story at the Black Spot." And he turned away. The lion let out a horrendous growl and all the cubs scattered.

The lion and his wife did not see their lodger, the lynx, for several days, except at a distance, the other side of the wall. The competition took place, but although the lion's *chef d'oeuvre* was played, the winner was a hare who had written a *Concerto for Four Formica Tops.* The conductorship, of course, was given to the ocelot.

The lynx came home to pack up his things and move them next door. "I've come to settle up," he said to the lioness.

She was ironing sheets: twenty-seven turtle-doves and two bluejays, engaged to sing in the Brahms *Requiem,* were expected.

"Why did you ever come here?" she asked the lynx.

"Very pleasant spot," he answered, all brisk and business-school.

"Can't you be honest about it, even if you are a lynx at heart?" she asked sadly.

"It was because you were lions, and I thought . . . Oh, it's all water off the duck's back now." And he left.

The lioness became debilitated and could not go on taking in lodgers and the lion had to go and beg the young lynx for his old back desk to be given to him again. But even that was filled by one of the cubs. "You can have the triangle," the lynx said, dropping cigar ash on the floor. "No one wants that."

As he waits for his cue, telling him to tap, once or twice during an evening, on the triangle, the old lion does not think about any new composition, but dozes and dreams of a past which has become all mixed up with old dreams of the future.

At home, his wife prepares his frugal supper. "Two can never play at the same game when one of them is a lynx," is the moral she draws from her own story.

The lion does not answer her. He has become very hoarse. For when it is a lynx who twists a lion's tail, the lion loses his roar.

Little Brown Burros

Two burros, a young married couple who lived on a farm near Oaxaca, decided to emigrate to Mexico City. "Life is very hard in the city for the likes of you," their master, a thick-fetlocked Percheron said. But the burro's hoofs were getting worn to the bone by the hard work of the farm and his wife, too, was becoming swaybacked before her time. As the burro looked about him, he saw that all the other little brown work-animals were in a similar condition. "We don't want to be field-hoofs all our lives. It is time we thought of our children's future," he told the Percheron. They were already parents to two soft-muzzled colts and, knowing the laws of nature, could expect more. Besides, a young mule from the city had recently been visiting the farms in that province, telling all the burros that they, having won the Revolution, were now entitled to better wages, better housing, free medical care, and free education for their young, if only they would take advantage of these benefits. So the burro and his wife put their blankets round their shoulders, and their straw hats on their heads, packed their few crocks into baskets, their water-supply into bags and, with their two foals frisking beside them, set out for the city.

When they arrived, one starry evening during the dry season, they were astonished by the cold and confused by the traffic. A long avenue, longer than all the furrows placed end to end at home, stretched out before them, interspersed with circles containing flower-beds and monuments depicting mules and burros in bronze. Burros in dapper uniforms stood on platforms, directing the traffic—though seemingly to no avail—which whizzed round these circles faster than a master's thong flicking a brown back. Otherwise, there were no burros to be seen: the avenue was crowded with wealthy palominos in English or North American cars. The two burros shivered inside their blankets, feeling conspicuous as well as cold. Indeed, they *were* conspicuous, for very soon they were ordered out of the way by uniformed police. The husband nudged the colts into a dark side street and brayed in bewilderment. The wife, being the practical one, got out the map the mule had given them and said, "We must make our way to Colonia Pocilga, where the hostel is. Here, he has marked it."

At dawn they finally arrived in a poor and tumbledown area, swarming with burros on their way to work, and in a foetid alley found the address the mule had given them.

After a few months they had settled down. They found two rooms in an adjacent alley; the rain-dampened plaster continually fell from the walls, the earthen floor was cold to the hoofs, and water had to be carried from a trough three blocks away, but there was a tiny yard where they could keep a few hens and a pot of oats. The father found work as a night watchman and the mother as a maid for some rich palominos. The colts went to school a few hours a day, for the rest, they scrambled and fought with others of their kind for parcels to carry away from the supermarket. The family increased until, in a few years, there were nine of them living in the two rooms, and the father's wages as *velador* were no longer sufficient to keep them in blankets or oats, so he took on a daytime job as well. The mother was not a very good *criada*, frequently getting dismissed from her jobs, so she became a washerwoman. The two eldest colts left school at the age of fourteen as, after that, one must pay fees for classes and this was not possible for them. One became a porter and the other sold lottery tickets in the streets.

At first the two burros had tried to find the mule who had told them, back on the farm, about the benefits due them, thinking that there was something they had not understood or, perhaps, some further effort they might make in order to achieve them. But they did not find the mule and one of their neighbors told them that he had been made Minister of Education. And one evening, on his way from his daytime to his night-time job, the father had seen the mule coming down the steps of some government building, carrying a calfskin briefcase and dressed in a silk suit—looking, in fact, just like a palomino. After that, he had not thought about the mule any more, or for that matter about much of anything except how to get along from one day to the next.

Even this, however, became increasingly difficult. The father developed a cough and the mother's teeth were troublesome, yet they could not avail themselves of the free clinic as attendance there required many hours of waiting which their hours of labor did not afford them.

Sometimes they would think of the past, dimly remembering their home in Oaxaca, and the wife would say, "It was easier to keep the place clean in the country," while the husband thought to himself that it had been an easier life: one rose at dawn there, but one could go to bed at sunset.

So their years passed. The eldest colt married and left them, the second was arrested for stealing lottery tickets. Other foals replaced them and in their turn grew up. The burro and his wife grew poorer and feebler, and now could no longer remember why they had come to the city.

One evening they saw an old mule walking down the alley, dressed in a coarse blanket like a burro. "Why, it's the mule!" the burro cried.

"I *see* it's a mule," his wife answered testily. (She had become rather bad-tempered since losing her teeth.)

"I mean *our* mule." The burro let out a weak bray and the mule stopped.

He was old, now, and grey about the muzzle. "Do I know you?" he asked vaguely.

"Back in Oaxaca," the burro said, "you talked to us, told us of the city . . ."

The mule hung his head. "I told so many."

"We thought you were the Minister of Education," said the burro's wife gummily.

"I gave that up," said the mule. "The Revolution was lost."

The burro gaped at him and pawed at the dirty street with one horny old hoof. "You said we *won* the Revolution, didn't you?"

The mule looked at him with sad brown eyes. "No matter where it takes place," he said, "burros always lose the revolution."

The Birds: A Fable
With Alternative Endings

After the war against the Painted Buntings had been going on for a while, a lot of birds decided that this particular war was unjust and in fact immoral. Some said this war was so bad it was like the time the entire genus of Passenger Pigeons had been wiped out. A few even went so far as to say all wars were immoral, but everyone knew they were just a flock of nuthatches. The crows, of course, being at the time rulers of the roost, along with some claw-licking rooks, maintained that there had always been wars, that to fight was bird's nature and anyone knows you can't change that. At the same time the crows feathered their nests and carried on with cawing-as-usual. This cawing aggravated the starlings and they started rioting because the war was taking the place of the campaign against the Cuckoo Clan. After a few months, Plymouth Rock hens started marching on Roostville, refusing to lay any more eggs till the war was stopped; presently a great many nestlings dropped out of mating-school and chewed up their draft cards, and a bunch of owls got put in jail for backing them up in public and inciting other young birds to do the same. From their cells the owls issued a statement they wanted all their fellow-birds to sign, stating that the war was unjust, etc., and that under these circumstances going to jail was in order. King Crow got fed up with all this screeching and decided to step up the arrests along with the war. A particularly wise owl, who was well known for his advice on hatching, and a whole flock of nightingales and robin redbreasts were indicted. Many birds in their winter feeding-grounds began to find that their daily larvae stuck in their crops. A mass meeting was called one night in the sunshine-capital of the West by a robin redbreast; birds of all sorts flew to it.

The robin held up the imprisoned owl's statement and put forward a motion that all present should put their clawmarks on it.

"Who," said the local owl, "doesn't see that this document is illegal? Just because those owls in Eastern colleges put it out doesn't make it any better. It's a matter of the law. Law is higher than Bird."

"That hoopoe in India said that if the laws of a country are unjust, then the place to be is in that country's jails," said the local nightingale.

"That was in another country," said the night heron.

"And the wench is dead," said the highbrow canary.

"What wench?" asked the tomtit.

"Order," ordered the owl.

"Signing this wouldn't do the least good anyhow," said the mourning dove.

"Useless," agreed the gander. "You think they're going to put a gaggle of unknown barnyard fowl into jail?"

The eagle put his talons together and steepled them. "It's a political matter," he said. "Excited statements like this one obscure the issue. We must use our voting power to get rid of the crows."

"Through the Crowing Party," said the rooster.

"How stupid!" said the night heron. "Through the Wading Party."

"*You're* stupid!" said the parakeet. "Through the Swinging Party."

"Order!" screeched the owl. "There's a motion on the limb."

"Well," said the goose, "I think I can do more good on the outside."

"What if all those nestlings and then those owls and hens had thought like that?" said the tumbler pigeon. "There wouldn't even be a peace movement!"

"Someone has to educate the public," said the hawk.

"There ought to be a world government," said the jay.

"It's a matter of law," said the owl.

"It's a matter of conscience," said the nightingale.

"I couldn't sign now," said the wren, "because I'm moulting. Maybe later."

"I've got a mate and a lot of nestlings to consider," said the house martin.

"My band is so shabby," said the snowy egret, "I wouldn't want to go to jail looking a fright."

"There's my tenure," said the puffin.

"It would *kill* Mother," lisped the cuckoo.

"Frankly, I'm yellow," said the yellow-hammer.

"Silence!" chirped the robin, as loudly as possible. "Where is your sense of solidarity with all those fine owls? What about the pledge you all signed to help end this war?"

There was silence. All stared at the robin. Every bird knows whose drop of blood fell on the robin's breast and made it red.

"We mustn't get sectarian—or mystical," said the eagle.

"The Pope would soon have a private line into the White Roost," the owl added. "I suggest we ask robin redbreast to stand down for the good of the peace movement."

The robin stood down and hung his head.

"Well?" asked the owl. "What about this motion? Who's going to sign?"

The owl, cuckoo, nightingale, canary, tomtit, wren, mourning dove, eagle, night heron, rooster, parakeet, gull, jay, etc., all perched stock still. Each one seemed to be waiting for somebody else to sign, but nobody hopped forward.

At last the little red hen made her way from the damp corner she'd been brooding in. "It's the same old story," she said. "If none of you other birds have any gumption, why, I will then."

She scratched her clawmark on the statement and ruffled her feathers. Two jackdaws stepped out of the shadows, their sheriffs' badges glinting in the moonlight, and arrested the little red hen on the spot.

ENDING:

Everybird went his way: the owl to get a good day's rest and the others home to their nests or feeding-grounds. The jackdaws marched the little red hen off into the night and she was never seen or heard from again.

ALTERNATIVE ENDING:

All the birds began to hoot, caw, quack, warble and twitter. "How disgusting," said the owl and opened his great wings. Leading the flight he, followed by the others in their hundreds, took off after the jackdaws and their little red prisoner.

"If you arrest one, you must arrest all," sang the nightingale when they got to Roostville, and all the others chorused it after him.

The noise was deafening and the jails were full. In fact, there was nobody left on the outside except King Crow and his rooks. These were sombre, boring creatures. "This is no fun at all," said King Crow, and declared amnesty. The war was stopped and the birds sent the Painted Buntings a whole lot of nest-material and mosquito-larvae so that their country could be built up again, and everybird lived happily ever after until the next war.

A Dried Mermaid

One by one the staff moles at Buena Vista Psychiatric Hospital interviewed the mermaid and got nowhere. They decided to call in Head Mole. They were having a staff meeting when he arrived. "What seems to be the trouble?" he asked.

They all started talking at once. "It's this mermaid," one said, while another exclaimed, "She won't cooperate!" and a third interrupted with: "It's her bosom."

The Head peered at them angrily. He had trained most of these moles himself. "Stop gibbering like a lot of gibbons," he commanded. He adjusted his glasses and began to read the reports which each of the staff moles placed before him. There was also one by the supervisor of nurses, Head Goose. He began with that. "Patient refuses to wear hospital issue stockings. Demands water all the time and I have to let her sleep in the shower. That singing goes on all night." Poor old Goose, he thought, she's been here too long.

He glanced through the other reports. "Subject has no sense of reality. Will not cover her breasts."—"Subject has a funny accent, sounds Viennese. Her bosom is too conspicuous."—"Subject immune to shock treatment. Anyhow, it's too hard to plug her in through all those scales."

And all had reported: "She disturbs everybody. And we can't get her music out of our ears."

Head Mole looked nearsightedly at his staff. There's something fishy here, he thought—but what? Mass hallucination went out with the couch. Aloud, he said, "You will all be removed from duty and given extensive tests. *I* shall now interview the subject." He left the staff room and went into an adjoining office. He spoke to Head Goose on his inter-com. "Send in your mermaid," he said, chuckling. He rubbed his paws together: he'd show these young staffers a thing or two.

"Send her? I have to *bring* her," the nurse's voice answered.

"Never give in to a patient's whims," Head Mole said.

"How can a mermaid walk?" she retorted.

"Nonsense," the Head replied—though to just what, he could not have said.

While awaiting her arrival, Head Mole continued reading the mermaid's case history. It began with several newspaper clippings. "Mermaid lands at Battery," the *Times* reported conservatively. "Mermaid refuses to live at Aquarium—'that's for *fish*,' she tells your reporter," the *News'* headline read. "Mermaid taken to Hollywood," the *Post* announced—"Censorship invoked." "Mermaid, back in New York, captivates Café Society," this paper continued later. And, more recently, "Mermaid sensation at Met as Thaïs."

Head Mole pushed the papers aside, pushed his glasses up on his forehead. "Yellow journalism," he muttered in disgust. He adjusted the desk lamp, placed his pen and a blank form in front of him, and cracked the knuckles of his front paws. Soon Head Goose opened the door. "Your patient," she announced, wheeling in the mermaid and leaving before the mole could tell her to remain.

Head Mole readjusted his glasses and stared. In all his years he had never seen such a bosom. A light piece of gauze from Pharmacy did nothing to obscure it. Then, too, there was her face. What green, slanting eyes she had. And her hair, black and coiling. Then there was her tail, thick and covered with glistening silver scales, ending with that delightful cleft fin which she lashed about so expressively. She reclined in her wheelchair as though it were a palanquin and sprayed herself from time to time with a cut-glass atomizer. The facets of the glass caught the light, but not half so dazzlingly as did her scales. Her hair coiled and uncoiled as though washed by wavelets and her perfect bosom rose and fell gently with her breathing. The Head realized how shabby moles were, with their stringy tails and dull coats, and he knew that he would never care about looking at his wife again—though she had four times the equipment of this mermaid, it was undeniable that she was flat-chested.

As the mole stared at the mermaid, regretting his myopia as

well as his puny tail, he realized that the silence in the room was filled with sound.

"What's that noise?" he asked.

The mermaid shrugged, causing the mole to look away hastily. "It is mermaid music," she answered. Her voice was as silvery as her scales.

"No music permitted in Buena Vista."

She shrugged again. "There is nothing I can do about it. It accompanies me wherever I go, as with all mermaids. It is the music of the waves, perhaps."

"Nonsense." But the music continued. He could not tell where it was coming from. She held no instrument, her larynx was not moving: some trick, no doubt.

Head Mole felt himself relaxing in his chair. He no longer remembered why he was here. The undulant music filled the silence. He turned his head and looked out the window. It was so dirty he could see nothing through it, but he thought he saw blue sky and white clouds.

"I wish I was a hawk," he said.

The mermaid's laugh cascaded like a waterfall. "You would have to change a good deal," she said.

Head Mole gave himself a shake. What in the world had he been doing? He turned his back on the window.

"It does not pay to be facetious," he said. "From now on you will confine yourself to answering questions. Where are you?"

"If you, a native of this place, do not know—who am I to tell you?" she replied gently. She leaned forward and sprayed her scales with her atomizer.

"What's that thing?" Head Mole asked.

"Surely you know that mermaids must be kept moist," she answered.

"Cover yourself decently at once," he ordered.

"It is against our tribal laws," she said. She flipped at the light piece of gauze. "I wear this only because of the drafts in this place."

"This is not some hotel where you can do as you please," said

Head Mole severely. "You must remember that you are being held here for psychiatric observation."

She laughed again. "What long, dissonant words you animals use."

"No more comments," shouted the mole. Why I'm positively thundering! he thought to himself—a veritable lion! He straightened in his chair and stroked his whiskers.

"What a lion-like roar you have!" said the mermaid admiringly.

Head Mole did not reply. He shut his ears to that confounded music, his eyes to that full, glistening bosom, and picked up his pen.

"Where were you born, and on what date?" he demanded, bent over his printed form.

"In the coral palace in the green depths of the sea," said the mermaid, her music at diapason. "In the year One."

"Nonsense! Give a proper answer, or I shall have you transferred to hydro."

"That would be lovely," she said, spraying herself again. "It's so dry here." She squeezed futilely at the bulb of her atomizer. "See, it is already empty again. Please fill it for me."

"No special privileges permitted at Buena Vista." He ignored her gesture. "Year of birth."

"About three million years ago, by land reckoning," she said, her music quivering about the desk.

About twenty-two, Head Mole wrote. Delusions of antiquity, he added. "Stop that damned humming!" he cried aloud.

"Oh, I'm not able to do that," she said. "As I told you, it goes where I go and will continue forever."

Delusions of immortality, he wrote. "Ever been in a mental institution before?" he asked.

"I do not know what that is."

Subject mentally retarded, he wrote. "Have you had previous psychiatric treatment?"

"Oh, that!" Her eyes sparkled, he noted. "Indeed, yes, by the Polar Bear, you know. We met at the Aquacade at Jones Beach, and he was most anxious to hear my dreams. He was a fine figure of a bear and I was happy to oblige," she said demurely. "Especially as he constructed a splendid tank in his office for me, with a sea-anemone couch."

"Dreams!" repeated Head Mole contemptuously. "Freudian quackery!" He rapped on the desk with his pen. "Answer my question sensibly."

"I cannot," she said, "because I do not understand it. And besides, I am becoming so dry."

Subject constantly creating diversions, Head Mole wrote—a sign of marked resistance.

She held out her atomizer. "Please?" she begged.

"No more diversions!" he shouted.

Patient will have to be removed, he wrote. Then he paused: but where? He riffled through her case history once more, noting how many institutions, already approached by his staff moles, had refused to admit her. "What am I to do with you?" he wondered aloud.

"I have seen enough of the animal world," she said. "I should like to go home now." Her voice was rather faint, and her music, too, seemed less audible. "Please do not keep me from it any longer."

Severe manic-depressive schizophrenia, Head Mole wrote. Indefinite hospitalization indicated. "But where?" he repeated.

She held out her atomizer again. "Please," she said weakly.

Patient must be removed from Buena Vista at once, Head Mole wrote. She disturbs everyone. He paused again, distracted by silence. It was real silence now, no more music, only a slight humming which vibrated around the wheelchair. "*Now* what are you up to?" he asked.

"Water," she gasped. "Or I shall shrivel."

Indeed, her scales were no longer glistening and silvery, her hair had stopped its undulant motion, and her bosom seemed smaller.

"Stop your nonsense at once," Head Mole said. Patient displays unique psychosis, he wrote. What shall I call it? he pondered. Morphophobia? Amorpho-philia?

The humming had stopped and a sound like panting was issuing from his patient. Her hair had become green and lank, her scales were the color of dust, and she was as flat-chested now as the mole's wife.

"Mermaids are immortal," she whispered, "but if you do not give me water, I shall shrink and dry up."

Before his eyes, she was drying and shrinking, until she was no larger than a specimen in a glass case.

"That's it! That's the solution!" Head Mole exclaimed jubilantly. He rang for Head Goose, and when she appeared he said, "Our problem is solved! No need to call any more institutions. Prepare a place for her in the specimen case."

The mermaid, shriveled up onto the seat of the wheelchair, was no larger than her own cut-glass atomizer, which had long since slipped from her grasp and fallen to the floor.

The mole rose and padded over to the wheelchair and looked down at his specimen with satisfaction. He already had a suspicious liver, a Manx cat with a tail, and three good, diseased brains: this would make his collection unique. He might even become famous!

"No more problems," he said. The music had stopped. His staff could get back to work. He looked at Head Goose. "What's wrong with *you?* Got a cold?" She did not answer. "Go and prepare the specimen shelf at once," he said briskly.

He looked down at the mermaid once more. From the tiny husk of her lips she whispered, "Why have you done this?"

"An obsolete thing like a mermaid, trying to set herself up in our culture—what did you expect?" he answered. He went back to the desk and put his form in a folder. *Case closed,* he wrote with a flourish. But as he turned away, he could not get the sound of music out of his ears; it seemed to go on and on, like an undiminishing echo.

The Purple Martin And His Cook

There was a certain martin whose wife was an extraordinarily good cook. All the other martins in that multiple dwelling envied him; they did not tell the approach of evening by the sun's rim in the west, or the slanting shadow of the old elm in which they had their apartments, or even by the bull frog's vespers down in the swamp. They knew the hour of nightfall by the delicious and tantalizing odors seeping out from one particular kitchen. During supper, they did not discuss the weather forecast, the day's profit in insects or the children's behavior. Instead, they would sniff and exclaim, *"Moustique marengo au sherry,"* or *"Escargots à la Hirondelle!"* and they would look contemptuously at their wives, pushing away a dish of cold midge and saying, "Why can't *you* cook like that?" The wives, naturally, all hated this great cook, this purple *cordon bleu,* and wished that she lived in a different tree. And so, when misfortune overtook her, they had to conceal their joy from their husbands.

The misfortune came about in this way. Once the purple martin's wife had successfully prepared a gourmet dish for him, she found that she had set herself a standard from which she could not retreat. Indeed, the time came when her own standards had to be surpassed: her husband's palate was like a child—spoiled, it needed more and more pampering. And so the martin's wife was at work in her kitchen from dawn till dusk—and after dark, as well, for her husband, puffed up with fat and a sense of his own importance, no longer helped with the dishes.

As time went by, the wife became worn out trying to keep pace with her own artistry; further, she grew moulting and dyspeptic from her daylong tasting for this or that flavor and from standing on her claws for hours on end. But the circumstance which eventually led to her mysterious disappearance and the subsequent scandal was this: no matter how great her labor or how brilliant its final accomplishment, her husband never expressed any appreciation of her cooking.

At last she could bear this no longer. For days she prepared a complicated dish, puzzling and tormenting the noses of her neighbors. When it was ready she set a steaming *cocotte* in front of her husband and removed the lid with a flourish. *"Gigot* of centipede marinated in oil, wine and garlic," she said.

She stood beside him, her feathers in a flutter. "Well?" she asked, as he took his first beakful. He merely gave a chirp and continued eating until the dish was empty.

"Well?" she repeated. "Did you like it?"

He wiped his beak with one wingtip and replied, "What's for dessert?"

Afterwards, after she had gone and rumors varied from the supposition that she had drowned herself in the bull frog's swamp to the one that she had flown away with an itinerant tomtit, after the divorce was over and the elm tree had settled into an odorless placidity, the deserted husband said to one of his neighbors, "What did she expect from me, anyhow?"

"Women are unpredictable creatures," the neighbor said. "Always wanting praise and bouquets of useless grasses."

"I don't see what more I could have done," the martin continued. "I always ate what she cooked, didn't I?"

Manifest Destiny

The mutant, thick-skinned, white water buffaloes journeyed by land and by sea and very easily captured all the olive-drab, colored buffaloes. After a certain amount of torture and shooting, the great sub-continent, with all its pastures, palaces and lush wallows, was entirely theirs, and for some generations the olive-drab natives accepted the notion that this was the mutant buffaloes' Manifest Destiny. The acceptance was not, however, without humiliation and a good deal of suffering. The Mutants, for instance, took over all the best waterholes, over which they erected signs reading *Mutants Only,* and in which they wallowed and played cards all day long while the Drabbians worked, parched, in the fields, though some of the younger ones were spared this, being employed at the wallows as fanners. Then, too, the Mutants made fun of the Drabbians' horns, as they themselves were clean-headed, and horns came to be regarded as a sign of barbarity. The Mutants' language was different from Drabbian, and they would not speak this outlandish (though native) tongue, forcing the Drabbians to learn *their* tongue— and then finding humor in the awkward way in which this was done. Even the signs over the usurped wallows were printed in the Mutants' cold, angular script. The Mutants' tails, friskily short, were without tassels, and instead of feeling deprived, this lack made them feel only the more superior. Some Drabbians even went so far as to "bob" their tails, but this did not alter the hue of their hides, so got them nowhere, except that they then no longer had tassels for brushing away the flies that attacked them all day long in the fields. Besides, tassels had been declared sacred by their god, Mu. Even though they were not supposed to worship Mu any more, they revered him as profoundly as ever, and tassel-bobbing

Drabbians were regarded not only as sycophants but also as
heretics.

It was the matter of tassels, in fact, which eventually brought
about the downfall of the Mutants. They took to buying up the
heretics' discarded tassels, or even sending the criminal classes—
panthers and pumas—out at night to bite them off the tails of
orthodox Drabbians, and then wearing them as pendants or
even as sash-ends falling obscenely between their legs. What
with flies, foreign languages and being done out of their best
pastures, palaces and wallows, the Drabbians took these tassels
to be last straws, revolted, and drove the Mutants out of their
country.

Such things of course are never possible without a leader. Here
in Drabbia an unusual leader arose from the people: a very thin
water buffalo named Mu-Waa, with crumpled horns and no
ancestral rights to a wallow, holding the strange idea that re-
volts could be waged without hoof-blows, locking of horns, tail-
beatings, etc., but simply by all the Drabbians sitting down
peacefully in the wallows and not budging. Strange or not, this
idea worked. The Mutants had become soft-hoofed and slack-
tailed from so much wallowing around in wallows. Even though
they sent to their homeland for some strong, lower-class Mutants,
the Drabbians managed to withstand all kicks and buffetings
without moving, until at last the Mutants were driven from the
country. Freedom! Mu-Waa immediately set about picking up
the pieces of government, and instituting reforms. For instance,
even the calves of field-workers were now to go to school, and
a policy of Wallows For All, whether one had ancestral rights
or not, was inaugurated. At the same time Mu-Waa decreed
that horns were not for fighting, that all beasts were brothers,
and that Drabbia would pursue a policy of peace towards their
warlike neighbors, the vultures.

But, as always in these cases, there was a dissident group.
Through the years the tassel-less or bob-tailed Drabbians had
managed to free themselves from field work and become the

Mutants' clerks or civil servants, thus forming a white-harness class. Now all this was changed. Mu-Waa did not care for civil servants and his policy allowed of no special privileges for anyone. Deprived of their ease and their status, the Bobbians became extremely dissatisfied. And they scorned Mu-Waa's peaceful policies, as well. "Peace is for the birds," they used to say, until one day they got together with some vultures and discovered they could start a horned revolt. For some reason they hated Mu-Waa more than they had ever hated the Mutants. "The first thing to do is to get rid of that Troublemaker," they said.

It was not difficult to pierce Mu-Waa's side with a sharp horn, one day as he was peacefully inspecting a school-wallow. After Mu-Waa's death, and while all his loyal followers were mourning him, it was not difficult to take over the country. The Bobbians, aided by some fierce pecks from the vultures' beaks, ousted all Tassel-tails from the wallows, closed their schools, and sent them all back to work in the fields. They erected signs over the wallows, *Bobbed-tails only,* and there they take their ease all day long, wallowing and playing cards and being fanned by tassel-tailed calves.

The vultures, however, now have their eyes on this sub-continent, so lush compared to their own craggy mountains, with fields that sometimes hold very large corpses and with good perching-posts over the waterholes. They watch the Bobbians taking their ease and becoming more and more soft-horned. And there is nothing, or so it is said, more sharp-sighted than the eye of a vulture.

Little Bear

The father bear and the mother bear, having struck honey, retired to California, where they bought a house with a patio, a palm tree and a barbecue. Little Bear, their son, elected to remain in New York where he lived a grubby existence as a clerk in a bookshop by day and an aspiring author in his cold-water flat by night. "The only salvation for an author is to keep his independence," Little Bear said, and he decided not to ask for any allowance from his father—fortunately, as none was considered.

Little Bear's life was one of deprivation and loneliness. The foppish Afghan hound who owned the bookshop sensed, without difficulty, that Little Bear hadn't two nickels to clink together in his frayed pocket (much less a bank account) and so when Little Bear asked for a raise, the Afghan simply smiled with his eyelids lowered and moved his head slowly from side to side, causing his silky ears to wave with discreet *panache*. Little Bear dared not press the matter, for his rent was overdue on the flat which he shared with a family of cockroaches, and he needed his job.

After three years his coat began to wear out and cardboard would no longer patch up his soles. The doctor, after Little Bear's bout of pneumonia, prescribed vitamins and a pair of galoshes. After some thought, Little Bear wrote to California, putting his pride in a pocket which, as we know, was otherwise empty. "Don't you know enough to come in out of the rain?" Big Bear answered.

"Your father's pained in his hind legs," the mother bear wrote, "and we've had to move to a house with a swimming pool, as the doctor feels a daily dip will be beneficial. The only

45

house we could find with a pool is larger and more expensive than our old one, which pains Big Bear's disposition. I am hopeful that the pool will be of benefit in that direction, too." However, she enclosed five dollars for Little Bear, with which he was able to lay in a supply of paper.

Little Bear was not particularly slow in his writing but, as he had only evenings and Sundays in which to work on his novel, it took him four years to complete it. Working in a bookshop as he did, he was aware that a book's completion was only the beginning of its travail. Therefore he obtained a Classified Telephone Directory and a lot of wrapping paper and sent his manuscript off to the first publisher listed under "A".

In exactly one week Little Bear was the recipient of a contract, an advance on royalties and a large lunch at Sardi's (East Side) which he was too nervous to finish. Anyone who knew anything about publishing was astonished—"It's a Cinderella story!" his friends said. Even the Afghan hound was impressed enough to give Little Bear a week's notice. ("Can't have writers messing up a bookshop," he said.)

"Dear Big Bear," the young author wrote, "it's a Cinderella story! My book is sold—and to the first publisher that saw it, The AAcme Company."

After four weeks or so, he got a reply. "Is it smutty?" Big Bear asked. "All the books I see around here are a disgrace—smutty."

Little Bear lived on his advance, still in his cold water flat and shivering through a winter in his old brown coat, and wrote his second book while his first was in preparation. This duly came out, sold most of its first edition and left Little Bear sixty dollars in the hole for copies given away to friends. While waiting for the second book to come out, he lived on the advance for that while writing his third, and also worked as a dishwasher in a coffeepot to pay for having his coat reglazed. When his second book came out he was neither better nor worse off than before, except that he got a raise at the coffee-pot and so was able to buy new soles and also to work on his next book with an electric heater in his room . . . And so life would have gone on for Little Bear, whose picture by now had been seen on enough book jackets so that he was sometimes recognized when attending a minor cocktail party, had he not come down with bursitis. How could he wash dishes with his right arm all crippled up? His boss said he didn't know, and gave Little Bear a week's wages. How could he hold a pen in such a useless hand? he asked his publisher. "Write with your left one, then—for all the money you bring in that's maybe what you *been* doing," the editor replied.

So Little Bear had to write to California again, where Big Bear's hind legs, according to latest reports, were much improved by his daily dip. His disposition, it turned out, was not. "If you can't make a living with your writing," Big Bear replied, "better give it up and get a job."

If an author's job is not to write, what *is* his job? the young bear wrote back. But he never got an answer to that one.

The Shaggies

One day the young dachshunds decided to grow shaggy coats. They all went to a pub called the *Sacred Cow* and hung around, waiting for their draft numbers to come up. A California dachshund of an older generation wrote a poem to them, beginning, "You came into a world of strife, boys, now where will you go?" They, however, had no ideas on the subject, except for those few who thought of Spain where living was cheap, until the more serious young dachshunds broke away from the group at the *Sacred Cow* and went over to the *Semi-quaver* where they had exclusive jazz and poetry readings. This group wrote very serious poetry in prose and their leader wrote one which began, "Atom bombs are a lot of crap," which was banned and became a best seller at the Afghan Bookstore. The California dachshund wrote articles about them, one of which made the Times Book Review. The young dachshunds' hair grew shaggier and shaggier, and they began to smell a little high.

The young dachshunds came from good homes where their parents were served special meals on special dishes; they were taken out walking by uniformed chauffeurs or at least by daily cleaning women; indoors, there was a good deal of culture lying around. Some of their fathers were very rich abstract painters, although these youngsters, during the tag-end days of free love, had been born out of wedlock and in Greenwich Village lofts.

One young dachshund, Jonathan by name, was a particular source of concern to his parents. He had been sent to the best preparatory schools, given only the right books to read and the right collars—simple English leather with button-down straps— to wear, and had never written anything but rhymed quatrains. Then, after but one year at Princeton, he had hitch-hiked to California and grown shaggy. On returning to New York he was a constant embarrassment to his family, what with his shaggy coat and bad manners and his crude verses that he insisted on reading at cocktail parties. Their concern was mixed with relief when he went off to live somewhere on the Lower East Side.

At first they made light of the situation—"After all, dachshunds are the only bohemians . . . Each generation has to make its own mistakes . . ." and so on. Soon their friends became so interested, in a smooth-haired, genteel way, in the younger generation, that Jonathan's parents dined out for months on stories of the Shaggies, as they were now called.

One night it so happened that the older dachshund from California, in town for a lecture at the Poetry Center of the AKC, was present at one of these dinners. So, too, was an old liver-colored bitch who had been notorious in her day for having had nineteen lovers, simultaneously and of both sexes, and then writing a book in dream-imagery about them. Now she lived in a dark flat in Washington Mews and walked with a cane which she used, her canine incisors having been extracted, for striking out at young whelps and potted geraniums. She was said to be writing her memoirs—in Basic English—and many a now-respectable abstract painter shivered in secret.

Jonathan's parents were out of things, this night, their places as experts on the Shaggies being taken by the California dachshund and the old bitch.

After her seventh martini Jonathan's mother broke into the conversation. "I bet none of you know the difference between *hip* and *hep*," she said loudly.

"Hip, hep, that's old yap now," the Californian said scornfully.

"Those Shaggies are a bunch of delinquents and should be locked up," the old bitch said.

"What do they do that's delinquent?" The visitor from California wasn't afraid of her memoirs: let her publish and be damned. "What do they do," he repeated, leering at her, "sleep around?"

"Huh," she snorted, "you think they *can*?"

"Or," the Californian continued with a look at Jonathan's mother, "drink?"

"They're all queers," said the host, a mahogany-red with a distinguished stripe down his back.

"No doubt your friend the Afghan hound told you that," the visitor said snidely.

"And they're all draft dodgers," the host added.

"We didn't have a draft to dodge," the visitor said, "in our generation. Not in peacetime. Did we?"

No one answered, as all were addressing themselves to the turtle soup garnished with kibbles.

The old liver-colored bitch lapped up the last drop and, twitching a nose which was as long as her pedigree, cried, "They're bums."

The Californian thumped his tail for silence. "How can one group of people be all one thing? Are they *all* queers, *all* draft dodgers, *all* bums . . .? Or is there a percentage of this and that among them, as in any group?"

The hostess, a black with a good chest marking, shrugged as though to rid herself of the whole issue, but Jonathan's father answered. "Certainly they're all *shaggy*," he said.

"Labels!" the Californian exclaimed. "I well remember how you," he said pointedly to Jonathan's father, "used to blow up when anyone said Chows were treacherous because of their purple tongues."

"I have since embraced the Church," Jonathan's father replied stiffly.

"Shaggies are sloppy," the liver-colored bitch said.

"We dressed up like porters and Apaches when we lived on the Left Bank," the Californian reminded her. Her neck hair bristled at him, but he no longer found that attracive. "Let's see what we can find that these youngsters *do* have in common." Jonahan's father began to growl softly, but before he could say "shaggy" again, the visitor continued. "Without prejudice, could we say they have their age in common?" He compelled silence with his steady brown glance, until Jonathan's mother replied, "Ours is twenty-one and his friends are about the same."

"Born in the late thirties, early forties. H'm." The visitor rumbled in his throat. "They *have* something in common, don't they? Something past that affects their future . . ."

Twelve pairs of long ears flapped at him questioningly, only the old liver-colored bitch disdained to be drawn. "Something past?" each repeated.

"A certain date in August of 1945, perhaps?" the Californian questioned softly.

All the dachshunds smoothed their coats and prepared to leave. The visiting Californian had spoiled the party, and the old bitch was impolite enough to snarl so. "Nobody knows what you're talking about, either, you old fool!" she added, giving him a mighty whack on the rump with her cane. "Anyhow," she said, "Shaggies are bores."

Jonathan's parents walked slowly through the night air. Pausing at a tree, the father said, "You know, dear, he meant Hiroshima."

"You mean the bomb? But what's that got to do with it?" his wife asked.

Jonathan's father began to walk rapidly, pulling at his leash, and his wife could hardly keep up with him. "*Dachshunds* are not responsible for what other kinds of dogs do," he said. He broke into a trot. "*My* paws are clean," he panted. Tearing down the street, he kept repeating, "My paws are clean, my paws are clean . . ."

Lambkin

The king of the wolves got married and in due time his wife presented him with an heir. This king was particularly powerful, as his realm was situated on a mountaintop overlooking a verdant valley entirely given over to sheep runs. Other wolves were envious of his domain and he was, of necessity, constantly on the alert for invaders or usurpers. To found a large family was vital to him; he was gratified when his wife's first cub was a strong male. He gave her a luxurious collie-skin blanket and handed out cigars to his cabinet. But when the cub was a couple of weeks old his coat began to get curly and his muzzle seemed suspiciously flat. The king kept his subjects at a distance, giving out that his wife had the mange, while he inspected the cub. The youngster had no fangs and his small feet were not only clawless but cloven. His coat was definitely *woolly*. The thing was a sheep.

Under cover of day, the king carried the monster down the mountain and threw it into the valley. Then he went home and threw his deceitful wife to the wolves. Rumor spread quickly and soon the king's subjects rose against him; howling that he was not worthy of ruling them, they tore him to pieces.

Down in the valley the sheep heard the wolves howling and ran to their folds. One couple, who lived on the edge of the valley, heard a faint sound coming from some underbrush. It being but a month past lambing time, their fold was noisy with demanding cries. "Hush, little ones," the dam said, "I believe I hear a ewe bleating out there."

"Or is it a cub howling?" the father wondered. They listened for some time, then approached the underbrush cautiously. There it lay, poor thing, an orphaned lamb. They brought it to their fold and set it down gently. "We will call him Lambkin," they said, "and raise him as our own."

Lambkin played and frisked, ate grass and bleated with the rest of them and in proper season reached puberty. All the other lambs gamboled contentedly about their valley, but Lambkin become increasingly dissatisfied. The sight of morning dew on clover no longer attracted him and the neighbors' daughters looked like broad-bottomed frumps. One morning he stole his mother's savings and made off for the city, where he bought a black leather jacket and a motorcycle. In no time at all he was head of a gang which, led by his wit and cunning, soon became the most powerful in the city. But after he had passed through his adolescence and reached sheep's estate, he again became dissatisfied. There were plenty of opportunities in the city—banks, advertising agencies and missile factories were full of junior executives who, like himself, must be wolves in sheep's clothing. But he had no college diploma or even a briefcase.

As he was standing on a corner one day, pondering his future, an old crow stopped beside him and began to read a newspaper. Lambkin saw the name of his native valley in a headline: *Wolves Attack Sheep*. "So what's new about that?" the crow exclaimed, throwing the paper away in disgust. Retrieving it from the trash basket, Lambkin learned that his valley had become exceedingly prosperous: for a generation the wolves, leaderless, had been fighting among themselves and the sheep, living in peace, had profited and multiplied until the sight of so many fine new nursery schools caused the wolves to unite and begin nightly raids.

"Opportunity knocks," Lambkin said. He gathered up his collection of weapons, put away since his gang-war days, jumped on his motorcycle and sped away home.

He hardly recognized the old place! The wooden folds had given place to cement-block split-levels, the gamboling green was overshadowed by a spacious town hall, there were clover-bars on every corner and, obviously, alfalfa in every pot. The populace was milling around the town hall, bleating for reassurance. Some bore posters: *Save our young . . . Make our homes safe at night . . . Get us guns or get out . . .*

Three old sheep were on the steps, trying to make speeches. Lambkin saw that one of them was his foster-father. "Sheep have always been peaceful. We must not resort to violence . . . Arbitrate . . ." he was saying. Lambkin saw that the old fellow had grown grey and paunchy. He roared through the crowd on his cycle, jumped off and ran up the steps, throwing off his jacket as he did so. His white wool gleamed the more brightly beside the dingy coats of the three elders. He held up a hoof for silence. "*I* have brought guns," he said.

"Lambkin!" the crowd bleated.

Within the week Lambkin had all the yearlings in uniform and drilling in the soccer field, while he himself, elected leader, collected the taxes and took over the elders' comfortable office. He called a few of his old jackal and hyena friends out from the city to help him with the drilling and collecting. At night the young sheep guarded the valley and if the losses were great, what matter, the reserves were still greater.

The wolves were used to swooping down on unguarded folds: organized warfare was too much trouble and they soon started preying on another valley.

The sheep prepared to enjoy peacetime prosperity again, but Lambkin remained as leader, collecting his taxes and keeping all the yearlings occupied with military service. All troublemakers were sent to the labor camp down at the carding mills. The sheep were sheared so often by Lambkin's tax collectors that they had colds all the time and became enfeebled. Lambkin rode around on a gold cycle and didn't care who got hit.

After about fifteen years of this regime the sheep decided to revolt. They formed an underground movement and printed some leaflets. "We are being fleeced," they wrote, "and our leader is no better than a wolf." They sent a spy to look up the town birth records, then issued a manifesto: *Sheep, your leader IS a Wolf!* They broke into the tax collectors' office and stole all the shears; armed with these they made a surprise raid on the town hall and, catching Lambkin and his cohorts with their guns down, rounded them up on the steps.

"Sheep are merciful," the underground leader said. "Therefore you will not be shot. You have the choice of internment in the labor camp—or being sheared and sent up the mountain."

The craven jackals and hyenas chose labor camp without a murmur, but Lambkin was made of finer stuff and started to make a speech at once. "Ingrates!" he shouted. "I saved you from the wolves."

"You're a wolf yourself," the leader of the resistance answered.

"No, no!" Lambkin cried. "I'm a sheep the same as you."

"That's what captured wolves always say," the sheep replied. "Get out the shears!"

Lambkin drew back. What would he do up on the mountain, without even a coat? It is better, he thought, to be a wolf in sheep's clothing than to go around naked.

"I choose the mills," he said. He knew there would be fresh opportunities in the labor camp.

Little Red Hen's Problem

One day Little Red Hen and all her chicks got sick in their crops. Everything stuck there and even when they didn't eat they felt sick; they were all rapidly wasting away. Little Red Hen dragged the telephone nearer her and first called up Owl and then her Freedom-for-Fowls Committee. Owl was in no hurry to pick up his bag and stethoscope and get himself over there, as he was in the middle of a game of chess with Eagle, and anyhow he was irked because he'd been counting on Little Red Hen to owlet-sit while he went to a tournament that night. Guinea-hen, who was secretary of the Freedom Committee at that time, was indignant. "Who the hell is going to manage our fund-raising Rummage Sale, then?" she screeched. "You are, then," said Little Red Hen. For the first time in her life her feathers, she noticed, were ruffled. But this didn't make her feel any better.

At last Owl arrived. He took all their temperatures and thumped their chests. "You've all got humanpox," he said. "Be quiet!" he hooted at the chicks, who had been setting up an awful squawk, saying how hungry they were. "You all have to stay in your roosts and you can't have anything to eat but rice pudding and custard," he said.

"How am I going to cook rice pudding and custard if I have to set day and night?" Little Red Hen asked.

"That's your problem," said Owl wisely.

The chicks never let up on their din nor their mother on her worrying. She decided to get up and cook the pudding and the custard herself, but when she got off her roost she was so weak she fell over.

Rooster, making the rounds of his wives, found her lying there beside her roost. "Well, what's the matter with *you?*" he asked.

"We've all got the humanpox," she answered faintly.

He drew away. "That's *catching*," he said accusingly.

"Only from humans," she said.

"What're *they* making such a row about?"

"They're hungry," she said. "And all they can have is custard and rice pudding, and where can I get those things when I can't make them myself?"

Rooster arched his neck at her. "Certainly you don't expect *me* to cook for you?"

The largest of the chicks spoke up, as he often did—usually to his regret. "Why don't you get one of your Old Hens for Freedom, or whatever you call yourselves, to make us something, Ma? They're always calling up and asking *you* for things . . ."

"Don't be such a wise cock," Rooster ordered, "or you'll soon feel the edge of my comb." He arched his neck again. "Well, I must be off," he said after a moment, and departed on his rounds.

Only a minute later the phone rang. It was Guinea-hen again. "Squab has a whole lot of nest eggs for the Rummage Sale," she said, "but there's no one to deliver them. What shall I do?"

"I'm too sick to talk," Little Red Hen said.

"Oh, dear—is there anything I can do?"

"Yes. We all need some rice pudding and some custard."

"I'll ask around. Well, I've got to rush. Right up!"

With the oldest chick's help, Little Red Hen got back onto her perch and lay there, her breast heaving. At once the phone rang again. This time it was the Leghorn down the road. "It's done!" she cackled. "My featherbed for the Rummage Sale. All nice and fluffy."

"I'm too sick to talk."

"Is there anything I can do?"

"Yes. We need some custard and rice pudding."

"Oh, that's easy. You can get custard all packaged at the Supermarket. And all kinds of puddings, too. Well, I must dash . . . Right up!"

By afternoon the chicks were too sick and hungry to squawk any more and Little Red Hen's voice was reduced to a whisper from fever and from talking on the telephone. Pea-hen, Goose and Duckling had all called to ask how to get things delivered to the Rummage Sale. At teatime a young turkey called, trying to sell tickets for the Right Up With Fowls dance. But none of these callers knew a thing about custard, much less rice pudding.

The next caller was Father Coot, from the Seminary on the hill. "I just remembered that I'm to help you at the Rummage Sale tomorrow," he said. "What time shall I pick you up?"

"I'm too sick to go," Little Red Hen said feebly.

"Well, in that case, I'll just take off and play golf," Father Coot replied robustly. "And pray for you."

"Custard!" Little Red Hen cried. But Father Coot had already hung up.

When Owl came by on his six o'clock visit, he shook his head sadly.

"All of you ravaged by fever," he said, "and weakened by hunger." He looked at Little Red Hen severely. "Why don't you pull yourself together and get some friend or relative to come and look after you?"

Little Red Hen shed a few tears over her brood. "There's no one who isn't too busy," she said. She sank back on her roost, after Owl left, to await her fate.

At twilight the bats who occupied the upper part of the barn began to wake up. One of them, known as Old Bat, had had a very interesting life. In her youth, when her wings were strong and her sense of direction perfect, she had been a well-known ballet dancer, famous for her leaps and *tours en l'air*. She had traveled all over the world and had many rich, even royal, lovers. Now she was beyond all that. Her radar didn't work at all, her wings sagged, and her pelt was mangy. She, who had once supped off larks' tongues, now could barely catch herself a mosquito.

She looked down pityingly at Little Red Hen and her brood.

"Is there anything I can do?" she squeaked.

Little Red Hen looked up in surprise. She had almost forgotten that Old Bat was there. Often enough, she had *meant* to go up to Old Bat's rafter and take her a little ointment for her pelt or help her bind up her talons, sorely calloused from being stood for so long *aux points*. But she had never got around to it. Bats were so different from hens . . . and she had always been so busy helping other birds and attending to her political activities. Now she felt even hotter than her fever was making her. But she thought of her poor brood, wasting away beside her, and answered, "Custard and rice pudding," in a barely audible croak.

About an hour later Old Bat slithered down a joist and tottered over the roost, carrying a large bowl of custard. "I'm sure it's no good," she squeaked, "as bats don't go in for custard, and anyway I had no vanilla. But tomorrow I'll get some rice," she added, slithering away.

In the morning, Owl found his patients on the way to recovery. "Little short of miraculous!" he exclaimed. He noticed the empty custard dish. "So you found some hen to help you after all."

"It was no hen," she answered, "but a bat."

"How disgusting," Owl replied. "Bats are rodents."

"There are more things on earth besides birds and fowl," Little Red Hen said. "And maybe they need freedom as much as we do."

Owl flapped his wings dangerously. "You sound deviationist to me," he said as he flew away.

The Concept Of The Cage

PART I

Once a week all cages in the Domestic Wing were opened, students were sent out to play in the disused Bear Pit, and every professor went to the Rotunda to Faculty Meeting. "These meetings," the Head often stated, "are true Meetings of the Minds." And indeed the Rotunda echoed with squeals, brays, bellows, baas, moos, neighs, cackles, etc., as the Chairbeasts of each department made their weekly reports.

On a certain Friday in the autumn of 197-, C.C.*, the Head, lay unsmiling on his specially-constructed tree-limb and announced, "No reports today. We have a grave matter to discuss." He stilled the grumbling, the rustle of prepared reports, with a brief hiss. "It seems that there is a serious Depression in the outside world."

"That cannot possibly affect our Temple of Learning," interrupted Goat.

"You are wrong," answered the Head. "I have received a Directive from Keeper, stating that we must cut down expenses in every way, and in every department. I now throw the meeting open to suggestions."

Never had the Zoo been so silent. "Well?" said the Head, growing a little dim from boredom. "If *we* don't come up with something drastic, Keeper will."

"Since Austerity began three years ago, we've cut down to the bone. There's nothing *to* suggest," said Donkey.

"Hear, hear," said Rooster. "I've already cut down to three wives. What more could I do?"

"I can barely keep myself in slops as it is," said Pig.

"I've got seven young ones to put through college," said Duck.

"--- --- ----," whispered Mouse.

"What's that?" asked the Head.

*Cheshire Cat

"Nothing," mumbled Mouse.

"We could cut down on the number of students," said Donkey. "My classes are too big, and they use up an awful lot of paper."

"Students pay tuition," C.C. said. "Don't be an ass!"

"I'm not," said Donkey.

There was another silence. "Well? Come on," C.C. said. "Keeper will be coming soon for some answers."

"You could cut down on the quality of your tree-branch, Head," said Goose.

"Yes, pine's a lot cheaper than oak," said Dog.

"But it wears out faster," said Cow.

"I have no opinion," said Sheep, as usual. "Put it to the vote."

"What vote?" C.C.'s grin reached formidable proportions. "You can't vote against *me*."

"What are we supposed to do, then?" Horse asked, stamping a foreleg. "Stand around here till we get fallen hocks?"

"I'll tell you what you can do." C.C. gnashed his teeth. "I'm to cut my faculty down to ten. That's my Directive. And that's what you can vote about."

"What!" exclaimed Cow. "I came here to vote someone *in*."

"Who?" asked Rooster.

"Calf," said Cow.

"*Calf!*" repeated Horse. "What use would he be? He hasn't even got a Ph.D."

"You'd only be bringing in another grass-cropper," said Sheep. "Not ecological."

"We're all right as we are," said Dog. "A nice, compact Faculty. With everything set up just the way we want it. Besides, it's Austerity."

"Well, I thought," said Cow, burping her cud, "I thought maybe we could all chip in a little . . ."

"Bullshit!" cried Rooster. "It's pure nepotism."

"You've got your semantics wrong," said Pig. "It's her son, not her nephew."

"All the worse, then," said Pig, "and at her age, too. It's disgusting. Besides, I won't give an inch of my wallow to anybody's son, nephew or anything else."

"Leave age out of it, you old sow," said Cow. "And remember how you tried to ring those shoats in on us. Scholarships . . ."

"--- --- ----," whispered Mouse.

"ORDER," shouted C.C., growing more distinct. "Can't you get it through your muttonheads that we're not hiring but firing?"

"I object to your ethnic slurs," said Sheep.

"Marxist!" Horse shouted at Sheep.

"Maoist!" Goose shouted at Horse.

"You're all Social-Democrat Liberals!" shouted Horse.

"ORDER!" shouted C.C. "You'll either vote one of yourselves out, or Keeper will come and do it for you." He gave a ferocious growl. "He'll fire the lot of you, I shouldn't wonder."

"But we all have tenure," whispered Mouse.

"That's right, TENURE!" The dome echoed with the chorused word.

"Tenure won't keep the university open," said C.C. "We can cut down, or close. So get on with it."

"But how?" asked Sheep.

"Best thing would be for one of you to volunteer to resign," said C.C.

There was an uproar, with all, in their various linguistic fashions, shouting at once.

"It can't be me," said Dog. "My discipline is the most important."[1]

"It can't be me," said Horse. "*My* discipline is the most important."[2]

"It can't be me," said Cow. "Mine is the most important."[3]

"It can't be me," said Goat. "Mine is the most important."[4]

"It can't be me," said Pig. "Mine is the most important."[5]

---

[1] Tailwagging.
[2] Galloping.
[3] Ruminating.
[4] Butting.
[5] Swilling.

"I could only follow someone else," said Sheep, "so it can't be me. And my discipline is the most important, anyhow."[6]

"It can't be *I*," said Rooster. "Obviously, mine is most important."[7]

"It can't be me," said Duck. "*Mine* is *inter*-disciplinary."[8]

"It can't be me," said Goose, "as mine is the most important of all."[9]

"-- ---- -- --," whispered Mouse. "---- -- --- ---- ---------."[10]

"It can't be me," said Donkey. "My discipline is the most important."[11]

C.C. faded a little. "You don't understand concepts," he sighed.

PART II

Keeper strode into the hall, his brass buttons gleaming on his blue serge and his keys jangling; his troop of soldier-ants filed in behind him.

"What's the decision?" he asked.

"None," said C.C.

"I thought as much," said Keeper. "Bunch of eggheads."

"I resent that remark," said Goose.

"So go ahead, resent," said Keeper. He motioned to his troop and they stood to attention. "As you can't seem to manage your Chairbeasts," he said to C.C., "we'll start with firing *you*."

"Oh no you don't," said C.C., and disappeared.

"Well that's one less, anyhow," said Keeper. "As for the rest of you, back to your cages." The soldier-ants herded all the animals into cages, some, in the ensuing clamor, being shoved into the wrong ones. However, as Cow remarked later, "In times of crisis, any cage is better than none."

---

[6]Following.
[7]Crowing.
[8]Quacking.
[9]Waddling.
[10]Nibbling.
[11]Braying.

Friends Of The Song Sparrows

One summer the Song Sparrow family had to move to another part of the country. A rookery had sprawled into the district which had been theirs, time out of mind, so Father Sparrow flew off to seek a new location. Every rural spot was very crowded with other birds who had also been forced to leave their ancestral trees, for similar reasons. But at last he found an ash tree in front of a deserted house, well-situated between a swamp and a brook, in an area still undiscovered by refugees, and where the neighbors were friendly. As soon as he had built a nest in the ash tree, he fetched his family, one bright July morning, to their new home. Mother Sparrow was at once visited by all the other mothers—Chickadee, Titmouse, Robin, Barn Swallow, even old Mme. Crow, who were cordial with offers of help. Father Sparrow, too, was visited and offered membership in the local Man-Watchers Club.

"We can't join until the Fall," Father Sparrow said, "much as we'd like to, as we are at present far too busy."

"Yes," Mother Sparrow added, "too busy. For, you see, we must teach our young to sing."

"Ah, of course," said Barn Swallow. He well knew that the Audubon Society had proclaimed Song Sparrows, since the sprawl of rookeries, to be an Endangered Species, as this was clearly stated on the fragments of a pamphlet with which he had lined their nest, the Society's chief concern being that the varied and exquisite notes of the sparrows' song should not leave the world the poorer for its disappearance. "Yes, indeed," he and his wife continued together, regretting that they had no such lessons of their own to give, "you must get on with your singing lessons, for that is your true *mélier*."

"We must do all we can to help," croaked Mme. Crow, putting the seal of approval on it.

And for the rest of the month, many birds often stopped in midflight to listen to the notes issuing from the ash tree. All agreed that the Song Sparrows' songs were unique in the community, in fact a great addition to it, and Robin, though jealous, even went so far as to turn over the patch of low grass at the roadside to the sparrows' use.

But in August the deserted house was bought by some bipeds, the ash tree was cut down, and the sparrows were again homeless.

"Everything will be all right, you'll see," the father said to the mother. "There are very good nesting-places in the apple tree, that elm by the road, and the willow beside the stream."

But the apple tree belonged to Robin, the elm—which was in poor health—to Woodpecker, and the willow to the chickadees. In fact, all trees were occupied and no bird would share one. Even the stone wall was occupied by Chipmunk. Worse still, the grassy patch was taken over by the bipeds and covered with lawn chairs.

But the sparrows' neighbors continued to feel helpful and friendly, and one afternoon called a meeting of the Watchers Club to discuss the sparrows' plight. After several hours of discussion, a committee was sent to visit the sparrows, at the roadside bush under which they were huddled, with some helpful suggestions.

"First of all," said Robin, their spokesbird, "you must realize that, however willing we are to help you, you must first help yourselves."

"That's right," added Titmouse, "you can't expect *us* to feed and nest you."

"You must not become a drain on the community," said Mme. Crow.

"But how *can* we help ourselves?" asked Mother Sparrow, thinking of all the occupied trees.

"We could give singing lessons, in return for nesting, to *all* birds," said the father.

"Who needs *that?*" answered Robin coldly.

"How impractical!" exclaimed Woodpecker.

"Why don't you teach Mosquito-catching?" asked Barn Swallow.

"Or Early-Birding?" asked Robin.

"Yes, something *practical,*" they all said.

Mother Sparrow put her wing over a shivering nestling. "But when we came here, you said singing lessons were our *métier* . . ."

"Anyhow, we have nowhere to nest," said the father.

"There's that old cuckoo's nest in the swamp," said Mme. Crow. "I can see it from my mountain. Maybe you could restore it."

"How could sparrows live in a *swamp?*" Mother Sparrow asked impatiently. "We'd get hoarse. And in any case, how could we peck up our seed in such a place?"

"Obviously," Robin said to his committee, "they don't *want* to be helped. They just want to *sing* all the time." And he hopped away.

After the Song Sparrows, already suffering from malnutrition, drowned in a rainstorm, the other birds were too busy getting ready for winter departure to think much about their former neighbors. One day, though, as Woodpecker was exercising his wings, he called down to Robin and said, "You know, I kind of miss their singing."

"Well, *I* don't," said Robin. "They were a useless drain on the community. No wonder they became Extinct."

A Hoard Of Nuts

The widowed though still youthful ermine decided to hoard her inheritance the way squirrels do. Before she could find a suitably hidden hollow tree, however, her stocks and shares of nuts had so geometrically increased that her glass-and-chromium lair was chock full and she was forced to go and live in her gazebo, a free-form collage of ratstails and cracked nutshells which was scarcely weatherproof. The riverbank economy had grown so affluent, what with the continual coconut-shelling of the beavers on the opposite shore, and the attendant boom in slingshots and cubtents, that it seemed there would be no end to this increase. Driving about day after day in her Topolino, she at last located a suitable site and immediately hired the donkey to come and transport her wealth, with two armadillos to accompany him and remain there as guards.

But as her beavers were loading Donkey's panniers, Old Fox, her legal adviser, driving by on his pink scooter, skidded to a dramatic stop.

"What on earth are you doing?" he asked.

Young Widow Ermine explained her difficulty, dabbing delicately at her nose with the flirtatious black tip of her tail, for she had caught cold in her free-form gazebo. Observing the fox's frown she added, "It's a very good tree, and safe as burrows."

"You're twenty years behind the times!" Old Fox exclaimed. "Nobody hoards their nuts any more. For one thing, you don't want to give half of them to those Rooks in Washington." He held up one paw to prevent interruption. "And don't ever think they won't find you, with their tame jackdaws prying into everything. But that's the least of it. Those Black Cats when they're all hopped up on hops and locoweed for a riot—there's nothing they like better than burning down a nice, big, maximum-security tree."

Young Widow Ermine's nose began to twitch and a tear rolled down each pretty, white, and still-unwrinkled jowl. "Now, now,"

Old Fox said, "nothing to cry about. We'll just put it all in a foundation."

Young Widow Ermine was puzzled. "Like under a lair?"

"No, no. A Foundation. We set it all up, tax free, and then give the nuts away to suitable Causes. I can be the Vice-President of your Board," he added, licking his chops.

"But what about *me*?" the ermine cried. "I haven't had a new car all year, and now I need a new gazebo as well."

"Oh, there'll be plenty for you. We'll just invest some of those common peanuts in some nice gilt-edged cocos—and then of course there'll be your salary as President."

Young Widow Ermine raised up her front paws and clapped them together. "What fun! When shall we start?"

"Now," Old Fox said. Instructing the beavers to unload the donkey and the armadillos to stand guard over the hoard, he sent Pigeon straight off to Washington, with the thirty-two required forms, all properly filled in; then he and the ermine went into the now comfortably empty lair to have their first board meeting.

"Well, what shall we do with all the lovely nuts?" he asked.

"Do you know, I was going to do something with some of them to help out Hassenpfeffer—for I have always been a staunch patroness of the arts, as you know—but since having had to spend a few nights in *his* gazebo, I've lost interest." She thought about the most recent evening, too, that she had spent with the young artist and added, "Anyhow, he's a washout."

"You could always find another one," Old Fox said, "but foundations for the arts are becoming rather commonplace."

"I've long had a dream," Young Widow Ermine said dreamily, "of setting up a scientific laboratory . . ."

"Now that *is* more unusual. But to do what?"

"You see," the ermine went on, still dreamy, "it's always seemed to me regrettable that we ermines have to turn *dark* in the summer. Of course it's not so very dark—not black, or even brown—but still, it is *colored*." She leaned forward and put one snowy paw on Old Fox's right fore-hock. His whiskers bunched as he noticed how slim and dainty it was. "Just think," she went on, "if we could be white all the time!"

He thrust her paw away. "Madam, you are foolish. White is *out*."

"Out?"

"Out. You want those smelly Black Cats rioting against *you?*"

"Oh, but they are beautiful. Black or no. How can you call them smelly? So sleek they are, and so down-trodden yet so deserving." She jumped up, her eyes glowing. "Maybe we could do something for them!"

Old Fox looked at her with new respect. "Madam, you've really got something there."

And so was the cornerstone of Cashewnut Foundation laid. Soon every hollow tree on that side of the river was made into a gleaming new school, library or medical center, and the largest, a blasted oak, turned into an auditorium where ermines went to hear the Black Cats give history lectures and read aloud their poetry. Most of the poems began like this:

> Summer ermines are pale, pale pale,
> and winter ermines are shit, shit, shit . . .

but the ermines never grew bored, in fact applauded the poets continually and meanwhile grew bushy tails.

Young Widow Ermine never had a dull moment. The Black Cats were a new world to her, and in fact she had one or two very special friends among the young toms, whom she never found to be washouts in the least.

As the affluence of the riverbank increased, so did her stock of nuts, which arrived daily by donkey and were syphoned off, also daily, into the Good Causes of Cashewnut Foundation. Of course all this took a good deal of pedial labor, which required more and more beavers. POWs were plentiful and every morning Young Widow Ermine went down to the market on the waterfront and bought another half-dozen. At night they were huddled, crushed, into the tattered remnants of the gazebo; at dawn they had some birchbark gruel and then worked for sixteen hours unloading and reloading nuts. Their hair fell out, their tails drooped, their paws were lacerated, and they were lousy. At last, one night while the Black Cats were rioting only two lairs away, one of the younger beavers held up a bleeding paw and said, "We too must riot."

"No, no," said the old head beaver. "First we will take a petition to our owner. She is, it seems, a kindly soul. She has been a great benefactress to our brothers the Black Cats."

"If she's so great why does she treat us like this?" asked Young Beaver scornfully.

"She's so busy with her Good Works, I feel sure she has not noticed our plight."

"Nuts!" cried Young Beaver.

"Don't use that word around here, son," Old Beaver replied.

Too tired to argue longer, the beavers set about drawing up their petition, each signing it with a bloody paw-mark, and in the morning, after the arrival of Old Fox in his new pink Phantom and the start of yet another board meeting, the old beaver and the younger one set out for the Big Lair with their document. Nearing the entrance, however, they stopped as they heard the approach of the latest thing in sports cars, driven by Young Widow Ermine's latest Black Cat protegé. The two beavers waited while he soft-pawed inside, purring out the newest hit-tune, "How's your pot, Hottentot?" Then they slipped through the door after him and held out their petition.

"Mistress, your great-hearted interest in Animal Rights is well-known," said Old Beaver, "and we beg you to consider ours."

"Beavers are animals, too," said the younger. And *sotto voce* he added: "We can riot as well as anybody else."

"Beavers!" exclaimed the ermine. "Why, you scruffy things, get out of my lair at once. Back to your nut-counting."

"Not so fast," Old Fox said. He gave the beavers a calculating look. "This might just be a good idea." He glanced at the new young protegé and then turned to Young Widow Ermine. "Black is getting pretty commonplace. What's your objection, now, to these beavers?"

"Those teeth!"

"I suppose they could be straightened."

"Well, they're *brown*," she said.

"That old prejudice again? Still, they're not as dark as black, are they, so why not?"

"That's just it! They're not dark *enough*." The ermine wrinkled her dainty nose. "And look at those tails, all wide and flat. Why, the very idea, barging in here. Upstarts!" she exclaimed. "Upstarts! Even shooting's too good for them."

"Oh, I don't know about that," drawled the new young protegé. He drew out his double-barreled slingshot and executed them both on the spot. He reloaded and shot Old Fox too, just for good measure.

The Silver Swan

One autumn day at dawn, the silver swan felt her song coming upon her. As you may know, the silver swan sings a song of unearthly beauty, but only once in her life, at the time of her death. This swan had been gliding for many days without rest or food, high above the clouds, where there nothing to come between a swan and the dome of heaven except the color blue. In fact, the Swan had been looking down on the clouds, observing not only their shapes but even their contents. But with the fullness in her throat and a lassitude in her wings, she had decided that she would like to descend to earth and pass her last hour among her own kind. Gliding soundlessly and majestically toward the continent of North America, she saw a salt water pond surrounded by reeds and overhung by a few willow trees, where the moon would probably rise in a pearly path straight out of the water. Here others like herself would surely dwell. In the far distance, she observed a great aviary with cages shimmering like a mirage of glass as they climbed skyward, but this pond looked to be out of the way and protected. She came to rest on the water and glanced confidently about her. However, there are very few silver swans now anywhere in the world, and none at all near large aviaries.

Throughout the heat of the day the placid waters were empty; not until the hour before sunset, when the tide began to run out, did the pond begin to be visited. Then a few night herons, two cranes and a flock of stilts came in their different ways through the reeds and began to fish. Then the silver swan realized her mistake, but by now her wings were too weak to bear her away on a search for her own kind. They would carry her only on one more journey, her last. She rocked quietly, treading water and

thinking about her song. Though she could not leave it behind her
with other swans, she was glad, now, that the herons, cranes and
stilts would be here to receive it.

These wading birds were slowly and industriously fishing the
edges of the pond, intent on their catch. So far, none had noticed
her.

As the sun began to sink behind the pendant branches of the
willows, the swan felt her throat become swollen and vibrant.
She began to beat her wings on the water. "Farewell, birds,"
she called out. "I shall leave this earth now. But first I shall tell
you what I have seen in the sky." She raised her beautiful long
neck and gazed at the clouds, which she had seen that morning
from above. "The clouds are filled with the thoughts and deeds
of swans, herons, cranes and all who fly, even to sandpipers and
geese," she said.

But the birds at the pond's edge, intent on their fishing, continued to plunge their beaks into the shallow waters and did not
notice her. The silver swan raised her voice as much as her
strength would permit, and in the clear tones of reeds played on
by the wind, continued, "Every graceful flight, every pure song
or first innocent piping of a cygnet, is contained in these clouds."
Her sorrow at leaving the earth was forgotten in her joyful
knowledge that her song, too, would rise up to them. "But there,
as well, all our evil deeds—every crime or folly committed since
the beginning of time—are gathered. Until now," she said,
speaking as clearly as she could, "until now, the contents of the
clouds have been in perfect balance. But now the evil is over-
balancing the good. The clouds darken."

And truly, the afternoon was becoming dark, as dark as though
night were falling. But the wading birds had not observed this
nor would they, even if they had stopped their fishing, have
heard the silver swan for, as she was talking, a flight of gulls
had approached swiftly from the seaward side of the pond.
Circling overhead, they were screaming, "Herring! Herring!"

The cranes looked up, and the leader of the gulls cried, "There's a run of herring."

"But look at that black cloud overhead," one of the cranes said.

"Only a passing storm," the seagull replied.

"Herring! Herring!" the cranes called to the herons and stilts, and with a great bustle of feathers began to take off in the direction of the ocean shore.

"Heed my warning!" the silver swan cried out to them. "We must send our most beautiful songs up to the clouds or, being overfull, they will burst and all will perish."

But the birds were already at the far side of the pond and did not hear her.

The silver swan began to beat her heavy wings more powerfully against the water: her time had come. "Farewell," she called. She rose into the air, a long winged shadow in the darker shadow cast by the cloud. Soon she was airborne and a song, unearthly in its beauty and heard only once in a lifetime, fell in silvery drops from the sky.

The gulls and cranes, and the herons, terns and gannets who had gathered there with them, did not look up when the swan flew over them, for they were busy diving for fish, nor did they hear her song, for the first thunderbolt, though held momentarily by her opening cadence, soon fell from the swollen clouds and engulfed them.

The Zebras' Revolt

The zebras held secret meetings every night under the trees at a spot well distant from the lions' waterhole. *Zebras arise!* was their rallying cry, neighed at first in muted tones. They stamped out secret signs with their hoofs at the edge of their own waterhole: "Throw off your stripes! Zebras are entitled to as good water as anybody else!" There was plenty of mud there to stamp on for, it must be admitted, the lions had long ago taken all the best holes for themselves, leaving only brackish puddles for the zebras, so that, underwatered and overworked as they were, their ribs were like extra stripes on their sides and their manes were mangy. At the end of the month zebras not only from all over the suburbs but even from the city had joined the nightly meetings. "Why should zebras be chauffeurs all their lives, for generation after generation, while the lions loll around in the back seats of limousines?" their leader cried.

Soon, armed with nothing but their hoofs and their high courage, they attacked the lions at their waterholes, one moonless night, and a bloody battle ensued, during which the lives of many young colts were ended. But the lions were fat and effete; after a season of guerilla warfare and several more fierce battles, the lions were driven from their waterholes and the zebras took them over.

At the same time—ideas often traveling faster than eagles— the zebras on another continent, in a southern hemisphere, felt the sap of revolt rising in them. These zebras' circumstances, though different from those of their distant brothers, were no better. Not only lions, but monkeys, baboons and even giraffes had taken all the best grazing spots for themselves. True, these zebras could frisk about on the *veldt,* but only in certain spots which became constantly smaller and were hemmed in by barbed wire. The grazing became so poor that some had to migrate and become beasts of burden for baboons. These zebras, too, revolted, and after many moons of fierce battle they, too, won and were at last masters of the *veldt*.

After the passing of several foaling seasons, when the zebras had grown well-fleshed and thick-maned, an intellectual zebra on the northern continent decided to inaugurate an Exchange Plan. "It's time we got to know our brothers across the sea," he announced. "We will send artists and writers to them and they can send agricultural experts to us, which will be of benefit to both nations." Praise from government circles set the seal of approval. The intellectual zebra at once boarded an Auk and flew to the other continent.

If he had expected (and, no doubt, he had) to be greeted, on landing, by fanfares and loud hoofbeats, he was disappointed. The southern zebras were lined up on the field to meet him, but he was greeted with silence. He raised one hoof and said, "Greetings, from your brothers across the seas." He was very moved by his words; his eyes filled with tears and a lump in his throat prevented further speech. However, his thoughts continued and he said to himself: "An historic moment."

The other zebras did not answer his greeting; at last, their leader stepped forward and asked, "Why have you come?"

"Surely the message sent by Air Pigeon explained that!" the visitor exclaimed.

The leader stepped nearer and the two animals were able to scrutinize each other more closely. The leader was a powerful figure with heavy shoulders and wiry tailhairs. "We are even different in appearance," he said slowly.

"What's that got to do with anything?" the intellectual zebra replied.

"Your stripes are so ill-defined," said the leader of the southern zebras. "And your tail—how strange!—it is quite smooth, with just that little tassel of hair at the end." He switched his own tail. "I suppose, living in households with lions, as your race did, certain regrettable incidents were bound to occur . . ." He shook his mane pityingly.

The foreign zebra pawed the ground impatiently. "Let's cut the chit-chat," he said, "and get out of this sun. I could do with a cool drink while we discuss the Exchange Program."

"There's nothing to discuss," the southern zebra replied. "We shall never allow our citizens to go to your country where their blood, too, might be polluted."

"But we are all brothers!" the other zebra, in great distress, cried.

"Oh, I wouldn't say that," the southern zebra answered "How could we be? For your race were . . . *chauffeurs.*"

Ears drooping and tongue parched with thirst, the zebra from overseas climbed again onto the auk's back and said, "Home!"

The auk laughed to himself as he took off, for, he thought, all animals in the world, except auks, are born to be chauffeurs.

The Jewel
And The Deerstalkers

"As everyone knows," the hind said to her son, "deer were always the poets of the world, back into the mists of antiquity. Especially us red deer who live on the mountain-tops."

"Then why aren't we poets now?" her son asked. "Instead of only rifle-fodder?"

It was time for him to go down the mountain now, for he had reached his majority, and armed only with his antlers and his swift long legs, pit himself against the alien race of deerstalkers, who were slow and cumbersome on their hind legs but whose buckshot was swifter than the flight of a butterfly, and who were often dressed in hides not their own, but those of the buck's older brothers.

"Why?" he repeated, as his peers, it being their season of conscription, were asking all over the mountain on that particular bright autumn morning.

"It's the law," the hind answered.

"Why?" he asked for the third time.

"The old bucks have decided, and they know best. Your father died a hero's death; you have to brace up and be a buck now, and be worthy of him." But I wish you'd been born with only three legs, she said to herself.

"I still don't understand," the youngster replied. "Where did the poetry go, and why must we get shot?"

"Because of the moufflon," his mother answered.

"What's a moufflon? I never heard of it."

"Not so loud. There are some things that we are forbidden to speak of. And not it, him. Them. They are the fleetest of all the mountain-dwellers. They live on the ridge itself, leaping from crag to crag, and surveying the earth below them."

"Live higher than us?" The young buck tossed his antlers—awkwardly, for they were still quite new.

"Live—or lived," whispered his mother. "Nobody's seen one for a couple of ages." She began to nibble the bark of the birch tree which grew over their home.

"Even so, what did they have to do with us?"

"It was their jewel. The jewel that grows in their breasts. A deer had only to touch it, and he became a poet. And safe, too, from the deerstalkers here on this mountain."

"Why did we stop doing that, then?"

His mother sighed and turned away from the birch-bark. "Nobody can find a moufflon any more."

"Well, *I* can," said the young buck.

He set off that very moment, not heeding his mother's cries of remonstrance, for the highest crag of the deer's mountain. After he had gone, a great bell and cry was set up by the elders: the young buck was declared a deserter, and a reward of one hundred pieces of oak-bark was offered for his capture.

A week later, sore in hoof and rump, with his handsome mottled breast scratched up and the tip of one antler chipped, he limped back, one midnight, to his ancestral tree. He was winded and could not answer his mother's anxious questions. Quickly she warmed up some bark broth for him and, when he had revived a little, she said, "I hope your quest was successful, for otherwise you'll be sent to prison."

"It was not," he said, his voice quavering. "All the moufflons are dead."

When the hind asked how he knew that, he answered, "I saw their bodies, lying lifeless on one crag after another. What's more, their breasts were torn open, and the jewels were gone."

"Gone? Who could have taken them?" Her large brown eyes filled with tears.

"The deerstalkers," he answered. "The oldest moufflon was still alive, you see, though only just, and he told me. The deerstalkers, he said, are great traders, and have many needs. They are no longer satisfied with the barter of deerskin jackets and fine polished antlers. Somehow they learned the moufflons' secret, and so they hunted them down, every one, and raped them of their precious jewels."

The hind trembled on her delicate legs. "I suppose they too wanted to become poets," she said. "But now they have killed the source . . ."

"Poets!" her son snorted. "Not at all! They wanted to sell the jewels for what they call money. Or so the old moufflon told me just before he died."

His mother looked at him quizzically. Money? What was that? —Had he actually seen a moufflon? or was he making up this story? "But what would anyone do with the jewel, after giving the deerstalkers this money for it? Do *they* make poetry out of it?"

The young buck stamped his hoof impatiently. "You've certainly led a sheltered life, mother. They use it to make something called perfume. To hide their smell. Haven't you ever noticed how terrible they smell?"

But the hind was no longer paying attention; instead, she was sniffing upwind. "I smell it now!" she cried. "The terrible stench of a deerstalker.—Look out!" But even as she cried out her warning to her son and tried to push him aside, the shot came, faster than the flight of a butterfly, spattering open his forehead and ripping his antlers as he fell to the ground.

Lord Of The Plains

One Saturday afternoon a buffalo decided to take his son to the zoo. The youngster thumped his hoofs in clumsy excitement, once they were through the turnstile, until his father gave him the shoulder and told him to calm down. "Now, where shall we go today?" the father asked, adding hopefully, "the aquarium?" —for he was something of an amateur ichthyologist.

"The monkey house! The monkey house!" the youngster bellowed.

"Peace at any price," the buffalo muttered. "Couldn't we pass through the exhibits, at least, on our way?"

"Oh, all right," his son said.

If the buffalo couldn't look at the fish, at least he could look at the exhibits. Some were stuffed, some mere skeletons, others only plaster models, so it was nice and quiet in there. The son was bored to tears with old dodoes, stuffed passenger piegons and whooping cranes, and the dinosaur's skeleton. However, he waited as patiently as he could and even read some of the signs giving the histories of these extinct species. At last he could wait no longer. He butted his father's shoulder and said, "Let's go."

"My, you are growing up!" the father exclaimed, twitching his shoulder.

"Whew!" he said, as they entered the monkey house. "How can you stand it?"

"What?" the son asked uncomprehendingly. He trotted past the cages, the ground shaking under his hoofs. He passed marmosets, baboons, and the chimpanzee shaking the bars of his cage, all without a glance. The buffalo was not displeased but he was growing breathless. "Going to a fire?" he asked.

"No, no," answered his son. "I'm going to see the Man. I heard about it in school."

At the end of the monkey house was a huge building, reaching up, as far as the buffalo could tell, to the sky. It had only three sides, the fourth being open to view, showing the public the building's interior full of little rooms with all different kinds of machinery in them, and another kind of machine that went perpetually up and down between the floors. Three buffaloes wearing guards' uniforms were standing in front of the building, patrolling it, and near them was a sign which read, *"Do not torment the animal."* Another sign told them, *"Man: an extinct Primate, in his natural habitat."* The buffalo and his son stared at the building and at last saw the man sitting in one of the rooms looking at shadows moving inside a box. None of the other rooms was inhabited.

After a time the man stood up and they could see how very odd he was. Small and hairless, with a white underskin that looked like curdled milk, he could only use two of his legs to stand on. He looked so unprotected, without any mane or tail or any hump to his shoulders, with, even, the best part of him exposed and quite tassel-less, that the buffalo felt embarrassed to look at him. The exhibit walked about its room in a restless way and then sat down again in front of its shadow-box.

"I'm bored," said the buffalo's son.

"You youngsters are spoiled these days," his father said.

"But what's all the fuss about? A whole place to itself—that puny thing. And it doesn't even jump around or howl."

"Puny it may look to you," the buffalo said, "but it was once lord of the plains. Of the mountains, too. And of the sea and the sky, as well."

The young buffalo was silent as they left the monkey house and he followed his father unprotestingly to the aquarium. For a whole hour, while his father looked at the fish, he was in a brown study. As they were leaving the zoo, the son spoke at last.

"And that's the last of them? Those lords of the plains and all?" he asked.

"The very last," the buffalo said.

"What made them extinct?" the son asked. "Were their brains too small, like the dinosaur's?"

"No," said the buffalo.

"Or were they hunted out of existence, like those cranes and stuff?"

"No," repeated the father.

"I bet you don't know," the youngster said.

"I do know," said the buffalo. "They wiped themselves out."

The son humped his back and looked stubborn. "That's against the laws of nature."

"Nevertheless, that's what happened," the buffalo said with parental finality.

As they trotted home to dinner, the young buffalo thought about all he had seen that afternoon. Man, he decided, had certainly been a unique animal.